現代英詩を読む

——エリオット，オウェン，ラーキンの作品を中心に——

中元 初美
Hatsumi Nakamoto

溪水社

前書き

　夕暮れの場末の通りを年上の女性と覚しき恋人のもとへ向かうプルーフロックの心情の表現の斬新さに魅せられて，現代詩の迷宮の中に入って数十年が経った。モダニズムやポストモダニズムの名はいまだに近くて遠いところにある。本書にまとめたものは，その間，一人でぽつりぽつり詩を楽しみながら，いや，詩とはいったい何者なのかと手探りしながら，3人の詩人の作品について書き綴ってきたものである。
　発表年には大きなばらつきがあり，重複している内容もあるがお許しいただきたい。また，和文のものと英文のものがあることもお断りしておかなければならない。
　ここに収めたものは以下の8篇に加筆，修正を施したものである。

［初出］
エリオットと言葉の錬金術　− Fragments of Mad Poetics −
　　名古屋経済大学人文科学研究会人文科学論集第35号1984年7月
エリオットのヴィジョンとサンボリスム　− マラルメへの帰還 −
　　名古屋経済大学人文科学研究会人文科学論集第37号1985年7月
詩形のエチュード　− エリオットのフランス詩とフォーム −
　　『言葉の地平』　英宝社（梅田倍男先生退官記念論集）所収1995年9月
T. S. Eliot's *Journey of the Magi*
　　− Journey of the Soul to the Still Point −
　　英語英文学研究（広島大学英文学会）第41巻1997年3月
Recognition and Ambivalence in *Marina*
　　英語英文学研究（広島大学英文学会）第47巻2003年3月
Wilfred Owen's War Poetry
　　− Pity, Beauty, and Horror of the Transitional Poet −

英語英文学研究（広島大学英文学会）第52巻2008年3月
Wilfred Owen の戦争詩と "the Instant Maturity Legend"
名古屋経済大学人文科学研究会人文科学論集第89号2012年3月
Another Mask ‐ In the Case of Philip Larkin ‐
市邨学園短期大学開学30周年記念論集1996年2月

もくじ

前書き ……………………………………………………………………… i

第一章　T. S. エリオット

1 − 1．エリオットと言葉の錬金術
　　　　——Fragments of Mad Poetics—— …………………………… 5

1 − 2．エリオットのヴィジョンとサンボリスム
　　　　——マラルメへの帰還—— ……………………………………… 38

1 − 3．詩形のエチュード
　　　　——エリオットのフランス詩とフォーム—— ………………… 60

1 − 4．T. S. Eliot's *Journey of the Magi*
　　　　——Journey of the Soul to the Still Point—— ……………… 82

1 − 5．Recognition and Ambivalence in *Marina* ………………… 95

第二章　ウィルフレッド・オウエン

2 − 1．Wilfred Owen's War Poetry
　　　　——Pity, Beauty and
　　　　　　Horror of the Transitional Poet—— ……………………… 117

2 − 2．Wilfred Owen の戦争詩と
　　　　"the Instant Maturity Legend" ………………………………… 139

第三章　フィリップ・ラーキン

3 − 1．ANOTHER MASK
　　　　——In the Case of Philip Larkin—— ………………………… 155

後書き ……………………………………………………………………… 171

現代英詩を読む
―― エリオット，オウェン，ラーキンの作品を中心に ――

第一章
T. S. エリオット

エリオットと言葉の錬金術
—— Fragments of Mad Poetics ——

序

　詩人としてのT. S. エリオットの生涯を考える時，'poet' という語の原義が思い起こされるのは興味深い。即ち，'poet' とはギリシャ語で 'maker' という意味であり，英語圏に留まらぬ現代詩の大きな特徴を示唆しているからである。一般に現代詩と呼ばれるものと1910年から30年にかけて全盛を極めたモダニズムの詩の運動は明確に区別されるべきであるが，19世紀から20世紀の今日まで概して詩における様々な実験の時代が続いているという事ができる。フランスの象徴主義の詩人やアメリカ人を中心に始まったモダニズムの詩人達による実験的な傾向は絵画や音楽の他の芸術分野にも生じている。様々にスタイルを変えながら飽くまで自己の主観に忠実だったピカソの絵は，エリオットの言葉を借りれば 'twisted beauty' と呼ぶ事が出来，伝統的な人間像のゆがみにはデヒューマナイズされつつある近代の病を見る事ができる。そこには美よりもむしろ危機感に訴える不気味な空間が描かれているとさえ言える。芸術に表われた実験的傾向と危機意識に注目し，19世紀末以降の社会と文学について上田保氏はオスカー・ワイルドを例に挙げ，次の様に述べている。

　　たとえば，ワイルドをとってみても，彼があれほどリアリズムに背を向け，自然や人生に対して，美や人工を愛し，「真理よりも美を愛するものでなければ，芸術の奥義はわからない」といいながら，いっぽう「社会主義のもとにおける人間の魂」のなかで，今日の社会を攻撃し，

私有財産が本当の個人主義を破壊してしまったといっている。…ワイルドの理想国はかなり空想的である。しかし、われわれはワイルドの一見きわめて審美的な芸術論を、彼のこうした社会意識とむすびつけて考えてみる必要がある。一人の資本家があたらしいすぐれた機械を私有する結果として、五百人の失業者が街頭になげだされるのだという、近代社会にたいする彼のするどい批判と無関係に、彼の悪魔的で逆説的な芸術論を考えることはきわめて危険なことである。ヒューマニズムとアンチ・ヒューマニズム、リアリズムとアンチ・リアリズム、現実主義と超現実主義のはげしい対立と交錯のなかにあるのが、現代社会のいつわらざる姿である。

したがって、文学においても次第に骨抜きになろうとする現実にたよらないで、リアリズムとは別の次元——つまり象徴主義や、知的、幾何学的、抽象的な方法によって新しい芸術王国をつくりあげようとする運動がおこってきても別に不思議とはいえないだろう。(「近代詩にあらわれた危機意識」)[1]

上田氏の批評は社会的な側面から新しい多くの芸術運動を理解しようとするものであり、世紀末の審美主義の芸術運動の背景にある都市における人間疎外の拡大を指摘している。このような社会と種々の実験的な芸術運動の中に青年期のエリオットは生き、彼自身の芸術のスタイルを捜し始める事になる。多くの詩人がそうであるようにP. B.シェレーやJ.キーツのロマン派の詩によって開眼されるが、ある意味で生涯象徴派の詩人としての趣向を逸れない。A.シモンズの「象徴主義の文学運動」との出会いは重大なものであった、と彼自身後に記している。社会的な視点から進んで芸術的、審美的観点から視ると、象徴主義は暗示（suggestion）の文学であり、神秘主義に属している。「夢の錬金術師」と言われ、事物を明らかに名ざすことは詩の喜びの四分の三を奪うことである、と述べたマラルメの宣言からも知られるように、象徴主義の詩には神秘主義と暗示の芸術としてロマン派の後継者としての色彩が強い。十九世紀におけるフランスの詩の流れ

は現実回帰に到るまでにはヴァレリーを待たなければならない。詩人の社会からの孤立，疎外の問題を抱えながら，二十世紀に入って，こうした状況の中で現代の詩心を詩う革命的な詩人としてエリオットは登場することになる。E.A.ポウ，ボードレール，イエイツ，エリオットという現代詩の系譜は批評家のよく用いるものであるが，現代詩の革新が十九世紀にすでにポウによって静かに開始されていたという事は，イギリス，フランスの詩の流れを越え，さらにはT. ハーディの詩に逆のぼってイギリスのモダニズムを見ようとする傾向も合わせて，モダニズムが基本的にアメリカ的なものである点で興味深い。象徴主義，とりわけラフォルグの影響を強く受けながらモダニズムの中心的存在の一人としてエリオットは成長していく。小論ではエリオットの比較的初期の詩を数篇取り上げ，彼の詩のスタイルの実験について考えてみたい。

1　仮面とピエロ

> 君にはわかるかね，ぼくはまるでからだが二つに裂ける感じだ……まるで第二の自我がじぶんの傍に立ちん坊しているみたいだ。じぶんはものわかりもよく，はなはだ理性的だ。だが第二の自我はまるでおはなしにならない阿呆な真似を仕出かさなくては収まらないのだよ。
>
> ドストエフスキー「地下室の日記」

> 「ぼくは生きる気はあるのだ。でもほんとうに理想はあまりにも融通がききすぎる！」
> 「それが理想だよ，名前そのものがそのことを含んでいる。その無意味さ以外に，ことばは偽る。」
>
> ラフォルグ　「月の出の前の対話」

エリオットは彼の詩人としての出発点においてJ.ラフォルグに負う所が

大であると述べている。「プルーフロック」がパウンドに激賞されたにもかかわらず，パウンドの一部改正の申し入れを拒んだままでアメリカで出版された事実の中には，エリオットの'maker'としての詩人の素晴らしさとともに，個性的，主観的な象徴主義の詩人達の一人であるラフォルグの主題に彼がいかに執着していたかを物語るものがある。エリオットとパウンドが詩のスタイルについて，初期の詩においてすでに衝突していた点に触れて，安田章一郎氏は次の様に語っている。

> エリオットの詩にあっては，ともすれば論理的，論述的要素が顔を出そうとする場合が稀でなく，むしろそれこそがパウンドとの相異ではないかとさえ考えられるのであって，すくなくともパウンドがエリオットの詩に注文をつけたのは，事実このような点においてであった。「プルーフロック」(1911)が『ポエトリー』誌にのったのは1915年のことで，足掛け5年にわたるパウンドの努力のおかげであったが，それほど肩を入れた詩であったにかかわらず，パウンドは「いや，おれはハムレット王子ではない」で始まるあの一節を嫌い，その削除を要求する口吻をもらしたことがあったのも，あの詩の中であの一節だけが多分に抽象的，説明的要素を含む異質的なものだったからなのである。エリオットにしてみれば，主人公プルーフロックの逡巡がハムレットの四大独白にみられるあの曲折のパロディだとすると，あの一節がぜひ必要だと考えられたのも当然だし，一方ではあれがなくても十分わかるというのがパウンドの立場だったのだろう。[2]

安田氏の意見は本来哲学者であったエリオットの思考形式と性質を指摘し，イマジストとしてのパウンドの詩の創造様式との対立を解明している。

エリオットの代表的な批評の一つである「伝統と個人の才能」(1919)において，彼は以下のような個性滅却論を説き，有名な触媒作用としての詩人の在り方を主張しているが，それまでには「プルーフロック」創作後，数年を待たなけれはならなかった。

...the mind of the mature poet differs from that of the immature one not precisely in any valuation of 'personality', not being necessarily more interesting, or having 'more to say', but rather by being a more finely perfected medium in which special, or very varied, feelings are at liberty to enter into new combinations.
・・・
...it is not the 'greatness', the intensity, of the emotions, the components, but the intensity of the artistic process, the pressure, so to speak, under which the fusion takes place, that counts.[3]

彼の詩論は詩人の不在,仮面の問題とも関わってくる。象徴主義の詩とフロイドの心理学で十九世紀から二十世紀の前半が特徴づけられるとするならば,次の様な発言はエリオットとパウンドの対立を理解する上で新たな興味を呼び起こす。

フロイドを20世紀化したグロデックによると,精神病の本質である自我の分裂は「俺は俺だ」という悪しき形而上学から生れたものだという。本来なにものでもないはずの「俺」を有として(それこそ)無理に定着することから来るという。ドッペルゲンゲルの現象はつまり誤れる形而上学だという。彼はこの19世紀的命題を20世紀命題に訂正して,「俺は『それ』(It)によって生きられている」といっている。…考えてみるならば,すでにランボーの天才が予見したように「俺は他者なのだ。」生れて死ぬまで人間は「それ」によって生きられた他者なのだ。人間は生まれたくて生まれたのでもなければ,死にたくて死ぬのでもない。[4]

「プルーフロック」におけるスタイルの問題は,即ち,仮面が破けて素顔が見えている点にある。詩論において完全に非個性説にまとめあげ

られるまでにはロマン派から出発し感情の生のままでの発露を避け，いかに現代の詩として芸術的にコントロールするか，といった大きな課題があったのである。そしてモダニズムの運動は大きな問題を孕んだまま進むことになる。ラフォルグの持つ象徴主義の影響を受けながら，エリオットがどのようにして彼のスタイルを創造しているか，彼の第一詩集(1917) の中のいくつかの小品を取り上げて考えてみよう。

Conversation Galante

I observe : 'Our sentimental friend the moon!
Or possibly (fantastic, I confess)
It may be Prester John's baloon
Or an old battered lantern hung aloft
To light poor travellers to their distress.'
　　　She then : 'How you digress!

And I then : 'Someone frames upon the keys
That exquisite nocturne, with which we explain
The night and moonshine ; music which we seize
To body forth our own vacuity.'
　　　She then : 'Does this refer to me?'
　　　'Oh no, it is I who am inane.'

'You, madame, are the eternal humorist,
The eternal enemy of the absolute,
Giving our vagrant moods the slightest twist!
With your air indifferent and imperious
At a stroke our mad poetics to confute —'
　　　And — Are we then so serious?' [5)]

第一章　T. S. エリオット

　　　「粋な会話」
僕は言う，「僕らの感傷的な友人の月よ！
いや　多分（実際，取りとめもない空想だ）
あれは聖ヨハネの風船だ
いや空にひっかかっているへこんだ古いランプかもしれぬ
哀れな旅人を苦難の道へと照らし出すための。」
　　　すると，彼女「何てあなたは脱線するのかしら。」

そしてそれからの僕，「誰かが鍵盤の上で組み立てている
あの絶妙の夜奏曲，あれで僕らは説明するのさ
夜と月光を。僕らの空っぽの心を具体化するために
音楽が聞こえる。」
　　　すると彼女，「私のことを言ってるの？」
　　　「いやそうじゃない，空っぽなのは僕さ。」

「奥さん　あなたは永遠のヒューモリストだ，
絶対なるものの永遠の敵だ
僕らの気まぐれなムードをほんのわずかにひねられる！
無関心と尊大な態度で
僕らの狂った詩学を一撃で論破するため」
　　　――「じゃ，僕らは大真面目というわけ？」

「プルーフロック」や「ポートレイト」より少し前，1909年に書かれたこの「粋な会話」にはパウンドのイマジズムの影響が見られ，次のようなラフォルグのとぼけた詩風が踏襲されている。

　　　　Autre Complainte de Lord Pierrot

　　Celle qui doit me mettre au courant de la Femme!

Nous lui dirons d'abord, de mon air le moins froid :
"La somme des angles d'un triangle, chére âme,
  "Est égale à deux droits."

Et si ce cri lui part : "Dieu de Dieu: que je t' aime!"
— "Dieu reconnaîtra les siens." Ou piquée au vif :
— "Mes claviers ont du coeur, tu seras mon seul theme."
  Moi : "Tout est relatif."

De tous ses yeux, alors! se sentant trop banale:
"Ah! tu ne m'aimes pas; tant d'autres sont jaloux!"
Et moi, d'un oeil qui vers l'Inconscient s'emballe :
  "Merci, pas mal ; et vous?"

— "Jouons au plus fidèle!" — "A quoi bon, ô Nature!
"Autant à qui perd gagne!" Alors, autre couplet;
— "Ah! tu te lasseras le premier, j'en suis sure…"
  — "Après vous, s'il vous plaît."

Enfin, si, par un soir, elle meurt dans mes livres,
Douce ; feignant de n'en pas croire encor mes yeux,
J'aurai un : "Ah ça, mais, nous avions De Quoi vivre!
  "C' était donc sérieux? [6]

「ピエロ卿のもう一つの嘆き」

僕をいっぱしのおんなつうにしてくれるはずの女よ。
わたくしはまず言うのだ，一番冷たいそぶりで，
「三角形の内角の和は，愛する人よ

二直角に等しい。」

そして，もし彼女が「ああもう，わたしはあなたをこんなに愛している」と叫ぶなら
「神さまは身内の者だとお認め下さるだろう。」そこでしゃくにさわって，
「わたしの鍵盤には心があるの，あなたがわたしのたった一つの主題なの」
　　　　　僕，「すべては相対的だ。」

じっと見つめて，その時！何と平凡だ，と感じながら
「ああ，あなたは私を愛していないわ，他のみんなはねたんでいるというのに！」
僕はというと，「無意識」に夢中の目を向けて
「ありがとう，どうにかこうにか，ところであなたは？」

──「もっと真面目にやりましょう！」─「そんなことが何の
　　　役に立つの，おお『造化の神よ』！」
「もうからない商人みたいだ」すると，また別の台詞
「ああ，あなたの方が先に飽きるわ，きっと……」
　　　　「どうぞ，お先きに。」

ついに，もし，ある晩，彼女がぼくの本の中で死んだなら
甘美に，僕はまだ自分の目を信じていないふりをして
言うだろう，「ああ，だけどこうさ，僕らは暮らしていけるだ
　　　けのものはあったのだ！
　　　　　じゃ，真剣だったわけ？」

エリオットの第一詩集は「『J.アルフレッド，プルーフロックの恋歌』と

13

その他の観察」という題を持っているが，現代詩の開始を告げるものとして興味深い。そこでは詩は叙情を詩うものではない。詩の創作は見る事であり，観察する事である。それには当然，現代詩につきものの批評眼が介入してくる。しかし，ラフォルグのピエロはラフォルグの仮面ではあっても，エリオットの分類によれば，第二の声に属し，装われた主観的な感情の吐露の色調を逸れない。F. R.リーヴィスはエリオットの第一詩集の完成度の高さに関して次の様に述べている。

> It is difficult to distinguish between attitude and technique : he was able to derive means of expression from Laforgue because of a certain community with him in situation and sensibility. The self-ironical, self‐distrustful attitudes of *Prufrock* owe their definition largely to Laforgue, and there the technical debt shows itself ; it shows itself in the ironical transitions, and also in the handling of the verse. But this last head has been made too much of by some critics : French moves so differently from English that to learn from French verse an English poet must be strongly original. And to learn as Mr Eliot learnt in general from Laforgue is to be original to the point of genius. Already in the collection of 1917 he is himself as only a major poet can be. [7]

ラフォルグに負うもの，それは「粋な会話」がモデルとした上記のラフォルグの詩においても多くのものがみられる。それは要約すればフォーム，あるいはスタイルにエリオットの強い共感を呼ぶものがあったという事であろう。「パリは私にとって詩そのものであった」と当時を振り返ってエリオットは語っている。ラフォルグの詩の中にある表現の数々の手段，即ち，ある女性への憧憬という主題，仮面の下での感情の吐露とちぐはぐな返事の組み合わせ，堅く抽象的なイメージ，口語の軽やかさ。もちろん，エリオットの詩の方には戯画化された傾向が強い。しかし，最も重要な点

はラフォルグのドラマチック・モノローグにあると言える。

 In his collections *Les Complaintes*, *Les Fleurs de bonne volonte* (a title which is a genial commentary on *Les Fleurs du mal*) and above all the unfinished *Derniers Vers* (a kind of verse-novel), Laforgue invented a new kind of dramatic monologue, close to common speech and reflecting his interest in German theories of the Unconcious.
   ・・・
 It is fortunate that Eliot took his monologue form from Laforgue rather than Browning, as it helped him both in his apprenticeship to the drama and his exploration of new verse forms.As he said himself, his free verse 'in 1908 or 1909 was directly drawn from the study of Laforgue together with the later Elizabethan drama'.[8]

後年,ドラマという劇的空間の中に生み出される詩の審美的創造に向かうエリオットの萌芽がすでにここにある。彼にとって詩とは主観的な情緒の吐露から逃れる事に始まり,最終的に劇場の中で登場人物の中から引き出されるものでなければならない。彼の言う詩における第三の声とは詩人から独立した登場人物のものである。そして,そのためには,

 In a play, an author must have divided loyalties ;
 he must sympathize with characters who may be in
 no way sympathetic to each other.[9]

と彼は述べている。ラフォルグのピエロ,即ち,仮面の下の嘆きにエリオットが見たもの,それはパウンドの創造したペルソナであり,第二の声であった。そして,それはやがて劇の中に吸収され,独立した登場人物の劇中で発っせられる劇の本質的要素として高められ,発展させられなければなら

ない。エリオットのピエロは仮面を取って，独立した登場人物としての舞台を待っていた，と言う事が出来るであろう。エリオットが学生時代からラフォルグの影響を受けてその詩風をまねていた事は，エリオットの死後，1967年に夫人によって刊行された詩集からも知る事が出来る。

Humouresque
(AFTER J. LAFORGUE)

One of my marionettes is dead,
Though not yet tired of the game—
But weak in body as in head,
(A jumping—jack has such a frame).

But this deceased marionette
I rather liked:a common face,
(The kind of face that we forget)
Pinched in a comic, dull grimace;

Half bullying, half imploring air,
Mouth twisted to the latest tune;
His who—the—devil—are—you stare;
Translated, maybe, to the moon.

With Limbos other useless things
Haranguing spectres, set him there;
 'The snappiest fashion since last spring's,
 'The newest style, on Earth, I swear.

 'Why don't you people get some class?

(Feebly contemptuous of nose),
Your damned thin moonlight, worse than gas—'
'Now in New York'—and so it goes.

Logic a marionette's, all wrong
Of premises;yet in some star
A hero! Where would he belong?
But, even at that, what mask bizarre! [10]

「ユーモレスク」
(J.ラフォルグにならって)

僕のマリオネットの一つが死んだ,
まだ遊び飽きていなかったのに―
頭と同様,身体も弱い,
(操り人形とはそんな骨組み)。

でもこの死んだマリオネットが
僕はむしろ好きだった,ありきたりの顔,
(僕達が忘れてしまいそうな類の顔)
おかしな,鈍いしかめつらにひきつっている,

なかば威張りちらし,なかば哀願するような様子,
この頃の歌に合わせねじまげた口,
お前は一体誰だと言っている彼の視線,
多分,お月さんにはわかってもらえるだろう。

辺土の他の用なしの物たちと一緒に
熱弁をふるう亡者たちよ,彼をそこに置きなさい,

「去年の春からの一番しゃれたファッション，
「最新のスタイルですよ，地球では，誓って

「何故，あなた方人間は授業がないのですか，
（わずかに軽蔑的な鼻のピクピク）
「あなた方のいまいましい月の薄明かり，ガスよりひどい――
「今，ニューヨークに」――そのように月は巡る。

論理，マリオネットの，すべてまちがい
前述の事項，しかしとある星では
英雄！　彼はどこの国のもの？
しかし，そこにしても，何たる奇怪な仮面！

次の詩は故意に伝統的な愛の詩形であるソネット形式で書かれている。

Nocturne

Romeo, grand serieux, to importune
Guitar and hat in hand, beside the gate
With Juliet, in the usual debate
Of love, beneath a bored but courteous moon;
The conversation failing, strikes some tune
Banal, and out of pity for their fate
Behind the wall I have some servant wait,
Stab, and the lady sinks into a swoon.

Blood looks effective on the moonlit ground―
The hero smiles;in my best mode oblique
Rolls toward the moon a frenzied eye profound,
(No need of 'Love forever?' ― 'Love next week?')

While female readers all in tears are drowned:—
'The perfect climax all true lovers seek!' [11)]

　　　「夜奏曲」
ロメオは大真面目でしつっこい
片手にギターと帽子，戸口のそばで
ジュリエットと，いつもの論争
愛について，退屈そうな，でも礼儀正しい月の下で，
会話が途切れ，ある調べになる
平凡な，そして二人のその後を哀れんで
壁の後ろに僕はある下男を待たせておくのだ，
刺せ，すると御婦人は失神して倒れかかる。

血は月夜の地面には効果的に映える——
英雄になって笑う，僕のお得意の斜めの型で
月に向かって血走った目が意味ありげにころがる
（「永遠の愛？」なんて要らない。——「来週の愛？」）
その間女性の読者はもれなく涙の海に溺れている——
「本当の恋人たちがみんな求めている完璧なクライマックスだわ！」

　気紛れな転調や極度のアイロニーは十九世紀末前後の英詩壇にはなかったものである。そしてまた，ここには詩劇やダンテの世界といった，その後のエリオットの進むべき方向を示すものが満ちている。
　ラフォルグによって触発された二十世紀初頭のハムレットの創造は，初期のピエロの仮面を捨て，プルーフロックという作者エリオットから独立した劇的登場人物として完成されていくのである。それは言葉の問題であると同時にスタイルの問題に大きく関係している。

2 'Twisted' サンボリスム

> ぼくは見た，あなたのふたつの眼が月の軌道のうえでぼくを
> いちべつするのを。
> ぼくは思ったものだ。そう，神々しいあのふたつの眼！でも
> なんにも存在しない
> 背後には！彼女の魂は眼科医のあつかう問題なのだ。
> 　　　　　　ラフォルグ「ピエロたち（短いが典型的な場面）」

> Jellicle Cats come out tonight,
> Jellicle Cats come one come all :
> The Jellicle Moon is shining bright ‒
> Jellicles come to the Jellicle Ball.
> 　　　　　　エリオット「ジェリクル族の歌」

ラフォルグにまねて紳士的な絶望を詩い，夢または幻想を劇的に完成し，一つの内的なドラマがエリオット独自のものとして高く評価されるに到るには「プルーフロック」を待たなけれはならない。ここでは，「プルーフロック」とほぼ同時期に，留学中パリで書かれた「風の夜の狂詩曲」とエリオットの象徴主義のおもしろさについて考えてみたい。

　　　　Rhapsody on a Windy Night

　　Twelve o'clock.
　　Along the reaches of the street
　　Held in a lunar Synthesis,
　　Whispering lunar incantations

　　Dissolve the floors of memory
　　And all its clear relations,

Its divisions and precisions.
Every street lamp that I pass
Beats like a fatalistic drum,
And through the spaces of the dark
Midnight shakes the memory
As a madman shakes a dead geranium.

Half-past one,
The street-lamp sputtered,
The street-lamp muttered,
The street-lamp said, 'Regard that woman
Who hesitates toward you in the light of the door
Which opens on her like a grin.
You see the border of her dress
Is torn and stained with sand,
And you see the corner of her eye
Twists like a crooked pin.'

The memory throws up high and dry
A crowd of twisted things;
A twisted branch upon the beach
Eaten smooth, and polished
As if the world gave up
The secret of its skelton,
Stiff and white.
A broken spring in a factory yard,
Rust that clings to the form that the strength has left
Hard and curled and ready to snap.

Half-past two,
The street-lamp said,
'Remark the cat which flattens itself in the gutter,
Slips out its tongue
And devours a morsel of rancid butter.'
So the hand of the child, automatic,
Slipped out and pocketed a toy that was running along the quay.
I could see nothing behind that child's eye.
I have seen eyes in the street
Trying to peer through lighted shutters,
And a crab one afternoon in a pool,
An old crab with barnacles on his back,
Gripped the end of a stick which I held him.

Half-past three,
The lamp sputtered,
The lamp muttered in the dark.
The lamp hummed :
'Regard the moon,
La lune ne garde aucune rancune,
She winks a feeble eye,
She smiles into corners.
She smooths the hair of the grass.
The moon has lost her memory.
A washed-out small pox cracks her face,
Her hand twists a paper rose,
That smells of dust and eau de Cologne,
She is alone
With all the old nocturnal smells

第一章　T. S. エリオット

That cross and cross across her brain.'
The reminiscence comes
Of sunless dry geraniums
And dust in crevices.
Smells of chestnuts in the streets,
And female smells in shuttered rooms,
And cigarettes in corridors
And cocktail smells in bars.

The lamp said,
'Four o'clock,
Here is the number on the door.
Memory!
You have the key,
The little lamp spreads a ring on the stair.
Mount.
The bed is open ; the tooth-brush hangs on the wall,
Put your shoes at the door, sleep, prepare for life.'

The last twist of the knife.[12]

「風の夜の狂詩曲」
十二時。
月光の総合に抱かれて
通りが両腕を伸ばすあたり
ささやきかける月の呪文が
記憶の路面を溶解する
その明確な関係を，
その区分と精密さを。

23

私が通り過ぎるどの街燈も
宿命の太鼓のように響きわたる，
そして暗闇のあちこちで
真夜中が記憶をゆさぶる
狂人が死んだ天竺葵をゆさぶるように。

一時半。
街燈がぺちゃくちゃしゃべった，
街燈がぶつぶつつぶやいた，
街燈が言った，「あの女をごらん
君の方に行こうか迷っている
にやにや笑いのように彼女に向かって開いているドアの明かりの中で。
ほら彼女の服のふちは
裂け，砂に汚れている，
彼女のまなじりは
曲がったピンのようにねじれている。」

記憶は高くカラカラに打ち上げる
ねじれたものの一群を，
渚に打ち上げられた一本のねじれた木の枝は
すべすべに喰われ，磨かれ
まるで世界がその骨格の秘密を
投げ出したかのように
堅くて白い。
工場の庭に一つのこわれたバネ，
その力はこめられたまま，パチンとはねんばかり
その形にしがみついている錆。

第一章　T. S. エリオット

二時半，
街燈は言った，
「あの猫をごらん，溝の中にはいつくばって
舌をちょろっと出し
ひとかけらの腐ったバターをむさぼり喰っている。」
そのようにその子の手が機械的に
ちょろっと出て，波止場を走っていたおもちゃをポケットに入れた。
私にはその子の目の後ろには何も見えなかった。
私がその通りで見たのは
明かりのついた鎧戸をのぞき込もうとしている目だった。
そして，ある午後水たまりの中にいた一匹のかに，
背中にフジツボをくっつけた年とったかに，
私がさし出した棒のはしを握っていた。

三時半，
街燈がぺちゃくちゃしゃべった，
街燈が暗闇の中でぶつぶつつぶやいた。
街燈がぶんぶん言った，
「月をごらん，
月は何の恨みも抱かない，
彼女は弱々しい目をまばたきさせる，
彼女は隅々に微笑みかける。
彼女は草の髪を撫でる。
月は記憶を失ってしまった。
洗いざらしの小さなあばたがその顔にひびを入れる，
彼女の片手は紙のバラの花をひねる，
それはほこりとオーデコロンの匂いがする，
彼女は一人ぼっち
いつも夜の匂いばかり

彼女の脳裏を往き来する。」
思い出が巡る。
日の当たらぬ乾いた天竺葵と
割れ目のほこりから。
通りの栗と,
鎧戸を落ろした部屋の中の女たちの匂いと,
廊下の煙草と
酒場のカクテルの匂い。

街燈は言った,
「四時だ,
この扉には番号がある。
記憶よ！
おまえが鍵だ,
小さなランプが階段に輪を拡げている,
登れ。
ベッドはあいている；歯ブラシは壁にかかっている,
戸口に靴を脱げ,眠れ,生きる備えをしろ。」

ナイフの最後のひとひねり。

詩全体に,'twist','memory','madman','skelton' といった語が散りばめられ,月光に包まれた青白い 'unreal city' がまるで一枚の表現主義の絵のように描き出されている。ラフォルグのピエロが石女の月という象徴に向かって嘆きをくり返すのとは異なって,ここでは直接の生の情緒がほとんど感じられない。ある街の夜の姿が,日常的な感覚を抜き去られて一つのイメージに収斂させられている。付け足しのように見える最後の数行は,これもラフォルグの詩の余韻であるが,月光の世界から日常の世界への帰還がある異様なひねりを見せている。イメージとは知的・情的複

第一章　T. S. エリオット

合体を一瞬にして明示するものだと言ったのはパウンドであるが,イマジズムの詩が静的な描写に終始したのに対して,ここではランプのつぶやきが時の経過を告げ,動的な空間のドラマが展開している。ボードレールやランボーの詩に見られるように,感覚の融合や意味の錯乱を生じた象徴主義の夢や幻想の世界は外界とほとんど関係しない精神的現実の探究を目差したものであると言われるが,エリオットは暗示や神秘といった効果の点で象徴主義を踏襲しながらも,日常的な時間を取り入れ,外界の現実を点描のように散りばめ,彼独自の詩のスタイルを築き上げている。それは時間ばかりでなく空間も含めた立体的,より現実に近い詩の構築となっている。『ビュビュ・ド・モンパルナス』という小説がパリ滞在中のエリオットの関心を引き,この詩に影響を与えたと言われている。パリの下町に生きる売笑婦の生活が聖と俗,抽象と具象の言葉で愛情こめて描かれている作品である。

　　われわれの身体にはどんな記憶でもすっかりしまわれている。われわれはそいつを自分たちの欲情とまぜっこにする。われわれはこういう荷物を抱えながら現在という時間のあいだを歩きまわり,いつ何時でもわれわれは一杯であろうとし,また実際のところいつも一杯なのである。[13]

上のような文章は,そのまま「荒地」の冒頭の詩行を彷彿とさせ,エリオットに深い印象を与えた事が容易に想像される。娼婦らしき女性は「風の夜の狂詩曲」の中にはわずかしか登場しないが,影響を及ぼした原作品とほとんど完全にまで異なった彼独自の作品になっている。

　フランス象徴主義の詩が伝統的な韻律やその他の社会的外面性に拘束される事から脱し,いわゆる純粋詩に向かったのとは違って,エリオットは現実社会に近い詩や夢を詩わなければならなかった。言葉が,イメージが,奇想が詩の中核となってオーラを生じ,暗示や幻想を生み出し,詩が現実社会から乖離してゆく時,生きられるものとしての時間とその時間の

27

主体となる経験は客体として私達から遠去かる。「風の夜の狂詩曲」はそのような象徴主義の傾向を持ちながらもエリオット独自の作品として異彩を放っている。

3　諷刺とナンセンスと

> Apollo hunted Daphne so,
> Only that She might Laurel grow.
> And Pan did after Syrinx speed,
> Not as a Nymph, but for a reed.
> 　　　　　作者不詳　17世紀英詩

'maker'としての詩人エリオットが作品において頂点に達するのはやはり「荒地」(1922)においてであろう。そこでは直接的，間接的経験が象眼細工のようにはめ込まれ，絵画の用語でいうコラージュを構成している。「荒地」の統一的視点はテレシアスに依るものであり，神話的方法と呼ばれているが，主題，構成，表現手段等についてまだまだ論議の尽きない作品である。エリオットの詩人としての発展過程を第一詩集において見てきたが，「風の夜の狂詩曲」と並んで'maker'としてのエリオットの特徴を一面において極限にまで押し進めた作品が「アポリナックス氏」(1915)である。

> 　　*Mr. Apollinax*
> *Ω τῆς καινότητος. Ἡράκλεις τῆς, παραδοξολογίας.*
> *εὐμήχανος ἄμθρωπος.*
>
> 　　　　　　　　Lucian

> When Mr. Apollinax visited the United States
> His laughter tinkled among the teacups,

第一章　T. S. エリオット

I thought of Fragilion, that shy figure
　　　among the birch-trees,
And of Priapus in the shrubbery
Gaping at the lady in the swing.
In the palace of Mrs. Phlaccus, at Professor ChanningCheetah's
He laughed like an irresponsible foetus.
His laughter was submarine and profound
Like the old man of the sea's
Hidden under coral islands
Where worried bodies of drowned men drift down in the green silence,
Dropping from fingers of surf.

I looked for the head of Mr. Apollinax rolling under a chair
Or grinning over a screen
With seaweed in its hair.
I heard the beat of centaur's hoofs over the hard turf
As his dry and passionate talk devoured the afternoon.
'He is a charming man'　—'But after all what did he mean?'
'His pointed ears…He must be unbalanced.'—
'There was something he said that I might have challenged.
Of dowager Mrs. Phlaccus, and Professor and Mrs. Cheetah
I remember a slice of lemon, and a bitten macaroon.[14]

　　　　　「アポリナックス氏」
おお　何たる珍奇！ヘラクレスよ，何たる不思議！
人間とはてれん手管の狡いけだもの。
　　　　　　　　　　　　　　　ルシアン[15]

エリオットと言葉の錬金術

  アポリナックス氏が合衆国を訪れた時
  彼の笑い声はティーカップの間でちりんちりん鳴った.
  樺の木の間で恥ずかしそうな姿のフラジリオンと
  灌木のしげみの中で
  ぶらんこに乗った婦人にあんぐり口をあけているプライアパスを私は
    ふと思い出した。
  フラッカス夫人の御屋敷の中で, チャニングチータ教授宅で
  彼はとがめられない胎児のように笑った。
  彼の笑いは深く, 海の中のもの
  あの海の老人の笑いのよう
  珊瑚の島々の下に隠れている
  そこには溺死した悩める亡骸が緑の沈黙の中を漂い,
  波の指先からこぼれ落ちる。

  アポリナックス氏の頭が椅子の下に転がっていはしないか
  それとも髪に海藻をからませて
  ついたての向こうでにやにや笑っていはしないか私は捜してみた。
  堅い芝土の上をやってくるケンタウルスのひづめの音を私は聞いた
  彼の乾いた烈しい話しが午後をむさぼり喰った時。
  「彼は愉快な人です」――「でも結局彼は何を言ってたのです？」
  「彼のとがった耳……気が転倒しているのに違いない」――
  「何か言っていた, それに挑戦しようと思ったのだが」
  フラッカス未亡人とチータ教授について覚えていることと言えば
  レモンの一切れ, それにかみ残された一個のマコロン。

この詩はB.ラッセル卿をモデルにした作品だと言われている。彼の印象風景の詩といったものであるが, 全篇ほとんど比喩である。たくさんの直喩と暗喩は極めて人為的に諷刺の色合いを強めていく。自然の感覚がほとんど完全に異質なもので塗りつぶされ, 登場人物さえも動物の仮面を与えら

れ，戯画化されている。神話の世界の住人や老人の海が生命力の源として背景を造り，G.スミスが説くように，エリオットの詩には珍しく力強いものになっている。

> In "Mr. Apllinax" Eliot's subject, portrayed as ebulliently vigorous, is mythologized to the point of absurdity. The satirist is good-humoured, however, not hostile; having been startled and a little awestruck, he is both defining his amazement and exhibiting his power to deal with it. The techniques of exaggerative contrast, Eliot's stock in trade during that period, find here their ideal material: an apparatus of mythical figures to be ranged against a modern. Images of Priapus, a foetus, the old man of the sea, a head grinning like John the Baptist's in Laforgue's "Salome" and a galloping centaur objectify resources of alarming yet preposterous vitality.[16]

このユーモラスな作品における比喩の効果として二つの事が考えられる。即ち 'absurdity' と 'unballance' である。人為性の生み出すある種の不安である。それはエリオットが再評価した J. ダンの詩の幾つかを想い出させるかもしれない。しかし，ダンの強靭な論理の連続性はこの詩の性質には見られない。エリオットの詩が成功するのは，奇想を用いながらもより大きな夢というわく組みの中で恋を詩った「プルーフロック」や，様々な引用作品や経験を点描風に並列しながら神話という壮大なパノラマの内に現代の不毛をとらえた「荒地」においてである。それらの底辺にはモダニズムの詩の特徴である混沌における秩序への志向がある。それらの傑作の周辺において「アポリナックス氏」という小品の人為性も考えなければならない。G.スミスは上記の引用文の後で，'"Mr. Apollinax" remains humourous rather than perturbing'[17] と結論づけているが，「風の夜の狂詩曲」にも共通する不安，ある種の乾いた狂気を完全に否定する事は出来

ないように思われる。そしてその狂気の裏側にあって,わずかに垣間見えるエリオットの素顔を通して,即ち象徴詩としては余分と見なされる最後の詩行の劇的なひねりや,海の中の緑の沈黙といったロマンチシズムの存在によって,モダニズムそして現代詩の置かれている芸術的空間と時間が考えさせられるのである。

　1939年,「おとぼけポッサムの猫行状記」が,エリオットの最後の詩集である「四つの四重奏」の創作期間中に発表されている。哲学的,冥想的な晩年の連作と軽い音楽的なナンセンスの詩との分裂はボードレールに始まった現実世界から遊離した詩の達すべき最終結果であったのかもしれない。エリザベス・シューエルはこの一見ナンセンス詩に見える「ポッサム」の中に捕え切れない神学の渦巻きを見るとしながら,

> このいわゆる小粒の作品には,「ナンセンス」詩人としてのエリオットの他の詩篇において彼に容易ならぬ困難を与えている愛と慈しみのすべてが見出せるのである。[18]

と述べ,一輪の薔薇を「ジェリクル族」に捧げるとしている。

4　結び

　'maker' としての詩人エリオットについて,第一詩集の数篇を選び,そのスタイルを考えてみた。それぞれ実験的な工夫が巧みに織り込まれ,いずれも妖しい光を放っている。それらはより大きなわく組みの中で,エリオットの生の悲劇的感情の詩的表現として完成させられていく。F.スカーフの次の言葉はラフォルグとエリオットのスタイルの微妙な違いを要約している。

> ・・・it must therefore be concluded that Eliot's most 'Laforguian' poems were not Laforguian in their essence. Laforgue, though in a

tragic predicament and intellectually oppressed by the pessimism of Schopenhauer and Hartmann, shows an inner stability. Eliot, like Baudelaire, had an overwhelmingly tragic, if not pessimistic, view of life, which he transcended only in the Quartets. This does not mean that he was inferior to Laforgue, but that he was more vulnerable, perhaps more sensitive.[19]

ラフォルグはある女性への憧憬を詩う事が出来た。詩った詩は悲劇的な色調を滞びている。エリオットの悲劇はある女性への憧憬という悲劇を詩わなければならなかった点にある。それは最初から救われない'overwhelming' の設定の下に展開される。そして，その悲劇を綾なす人為的な工夫をこれほど見事に引き受けた事実の中に特に初期の頃のエリオットの詩人としての独自性と悲劇性がある。

And I have known the eyes already, known them all-
The eyes that fix you in a formulated phrase,
And when I am formulated, sprawling on a pin,
When I am pinned and wriggling on the wall,
Then how should I begin
To spit out all the butt-ends of my days and ways?
　　　And how should I presume?[20]

様々な実験と技巧の駆使によってエリオットの感性が詩的に定着する時，彼のスタイルが築かれていく。そしてそれは周知のように，以後幾度か大きな転回を示すことになる。

　最近のTLSによれば，詩の世界においてポストモダニズムの混乱とモダニズムそのものへの郷愁が見られるという事である。[21] 新聞紙上に散見される詩のうちの一つの次の様な詩には，同じく生の悲劇的感情を詩いながらも，非常にシンプルな詩のスタイルと，より'discoursive'で

'undramatic' な特徴が見出される。

Perpuetual Motion

They're changing partners again, safely unseen
(Or so they thought) on the other side of the wall
Where death, dialing the defunct
Phone numbers you still know by heart,
Reaches an eternal dial tone.

Time out for a few last questions.
"Is there a unifying principle to these kisses and betrayals,
Some heavenly conspiracy that controls such accidents
So that they seem to make sense? Or are the players
Just pieces in a Jackson Pollock jigsaw puzzle?
"Does the malevolence of nature console us
Because, though innocent, we have never been good,
Or do we recoil in horror
From the grinning clown face on the back
Of a cobra's extended hood?
"No wonder we feel misunderstood.
You can measure our velocity but not our location
As we round the curve into the recent future,
Afraid to say what we have seen,
Alone and together on the way."

DAVID LEHMAN
TLS., January 27, 1984

第一章　T.S.エリオット

　　　「不断の運行」

彼らはまた相手を変えている，うまく見つからないように
（またはそう思っていた）壁の向こう側
そこには死がいて，あなたがまだ記憶している
死者達のダイヤルを廻し
永遠の呼び出し音を鳴らす。

二，三最後の質問のための時間。
「こういったキスや裏切りには統一原理というものがあるのですか。
そういった遇然を支配する何か天の陰謀でも
それで納得のいくような。つまり演者達は
ジャクソン・ポロックのはめ絵のボール紙の切れっぱしにすぎないのですか。

「意地悪な自然が私達を慰めてくれるのですか。
私達自身に罪はなくても，決して善人ではなかったのだから，と。
つまり，私達はずきんのようにふくらんだコブラの首の
背後でにやにや笑っている道化の顔に
ぞっとして縮み上がるというわけ？
「私達は誤解されていると感じても当然なのだ。
あなたには私達の速さは測れても，居場所はだめなのだ
私達は近未来へとカーブを曲がっていくのだから，
私達が見てきたものを口に出すのが恐いから，
たった一人で，またみんなと一緒に進んでいくばかり。」
　　　　　　　　　　　　　　　　デビット・レーマン
　　　　　　　　　　　　　　　TLS　1月27日　'84

エリオットの初期の詩との距離は，詩は時代を写すという事であろうか。

エリオットはラフォルグや象徴派の詩を踏襲しながら，自身の作品を'mad poetics'と相対化する目を持っている。様々な詩の実験を行いながら，マラルメに劣らないその錬金術の操作の中には，すでに，後の作品における多くの重要な要素が興味深い形で顔をのぞかせている。そしてイギリス現代詩における大きな出発点となっている。

注

1）上田保『象徴主義の文学と現代』(慶応通信刊，1977) 214-15.
2）安田章一郎『エリオットと伝統』(研究社，1977) 255-56.「妥協への道」
3）Eliot, T. S. *Selected Essays,* (Faber and Faber Ltd., London, 1972), 18-19.
4）深瀬基寛『深瀬基寛集　第一集』(筑摩書房，1968) p.359「現代の詩心」
5）Eliot, T. S. *Collected Poems 1909-1962,* (Faber and Faber, 1970), 35.
6）Laforgue, Jules. *Poésies Complètes,* (Éditions Gallimard et Libraire, Générale Française, l970), 85.　日本語訳については広田正敏著『ラフォルグの肖像』JCA出版参照.
7）Leavis, F. R. *New Bearings in English Poetry,* (Pelican Book, 1972), 62-63.
8）Scarfe, Francis. *Eliot and Nineteenth-century French Poetry* in *Eliot in Perspective,* ed. by Graham Martin, (Macmillan, 1970), 53.
9）Eliot, T. S. *On Poetry and Poets,* (Faber and Faber, l971), 94-95.
10）Eliot, T. S. *Poems Written in Early Youth,* (Faber and Faber, 1967), 30.
11）Eliot, *Poems in Early Youth* 27.
12）Eliot, *Poems* 26-28.
13）フィリップ作　淀野隆三訳『ビュビュ・ド・モンパルナス』(岩波文庫，1984) 11.
14）Eliot, *Poems* 33.
15）参考，中央公論社『エリオット全集 I』; Lucian: ルキアノスはシリア生まれのギリシャの諷刺散文作家（120?－180?）
16）Smith, Grover. *T. S. Eliot's Poetry & Plays,* (The University of Chicago Press, 1971), 32.
17）Smith, *Eliot's* 33.
18）参考　中央公論社『エリオット全集　3』月報3
19）Scarfe, 59.
20）Eliot, *Poems* 15.
21）cf.

第一章　T. S. エリオット

Here, an astonishing variety of avantgarde activities is subsumed by a deconstructive rhetoric of perplexing generality.The air of crisis such pieces stir up is frenetically artificial, and suggests that the real trouble is nostalgia for the golden age of modernism proper. Many of these writers seem to want to attend at the birth of something radically new, but some have already been waiting rather a long time. What is depressingly evident in this book is a deep, humourless hostility to art on the fashionable side and defeated withdrawal into curatorship on the other. Postmodernism is left looking like the mere backwash the words suggests, an epoch of unrestrained literary theory and complete unreality.
IHAB HASSAN and SALLY HASSAN（Editors）
Innovation/ Renovation: New Perspective on the Humanities
University of Wisconsin Press. TLS Feb.17 1984.

エリオットのヴィジョンとサンボリスム
── マラルメへの帰還 ──

　最近のRonald Bushの論文, *Modernism/ Postmodern: Eliot, Perse, Mallarmé, and the Future of the Barbarians* (*Modernism Reconsidered*, Harvard University Press, 1983) によると, 1926年にCambridge大学でエリオットが発表した一連のClark Lecturesの準備に際して, エリオットのマラルメへの関心が高まった事が考えられると言われている。論文の内容は形而上詩人に関するものだが, *Burnt Norton*におけるマラルメ流の詩の存在からもエリオットの象徴主義への関心が続いていた事は容易に推量される。エリオットがラフオルグその他のフランス象徴詩の模倣から出発した事はよく知られているが, その後, *Four Quartets*に到るまでその影響を跡付けるものは多くない。まれにやや批判的に言及される程度である。たとえばDonald Davieは*Dry Salvages*の最初の部分に触れて次の様に述べている。

> 'His rhythm was present in...' represents just that bridgework, that filling in and faking of transitions, which Eliot as a post-symbolist poet has always contrived to do without. From first to last his procedure has been the symbolist procedure of 'juxtaposition without copula', the setting down of images side by side with a space between them, a space that does not need to be bridged.[1]

　「彼のリズムは小供部屋の中にあった」という行はまさに橋をかける作業, 通過のすき間を埋めたり, 繕ろったりする作業を表わしてい

第一章　T. S. エリオット

る。それはエリオットがポスト・サンボリストとしていつもそれなしですまそうとしたものである。最初から最後まで彼の手順は「ケイ辞なしの並列」という象徴派詩人の手順であった。即ち，イメージとイメージの間に，橋渡しされる必要のない空間を置いてイメージを並べて置く事だった。

Danald Davieは，並列による 'invocation'（喚起）という象徴派の手法を踏襲する事にエリオットが性急すぎ，その点，詩として無理がある事を指摘している。問題の行は次の通りである。

> His rhythm was present in the nursery bedroom,
> In the rank ailanthus of the April dooryard,
> In the smell of grapes on the autumn table,
> And the evening circle in the winter gaslight.[2]
> 　　　*Dry Salvages*, 11-14.

> 彼のリズムは小供部屋の中にあった，
> 四月の戸口の繁ったにわうるしの中に，
> 秋のテーブルの上のぶどうの香りの中に，
> そして冬のガス燈のたそがれの輪の中に。

ここでは象徴派詩人達が目差した普通の意識以上のものを呼び起こすという事より，イメージの正確さと鮮明さによる詩の美しさに重点がある。さらには，語と語，行と行の相互浸透から生まれてくる静かなセンセーションや，詩句の効果の一過性という象徴詩の特徴はなく，より 'discursive' で，'undramatic' なものになっている。さきに挙げたRonald Bushによると，1927年までにモダニズムは亀裂を生じ始め，*Four Quartets*はポストモダニズムの先触れとされている。Bushはモダニズムの本質を自己というものの心理学的探究と象徴派の音楽の結合という点にみており，*The*

39

*Waste Land*以後、エリオットは、後者の詩の音楽性や 'incantation' (呪文)に重心を移していると述べている。では、ラフォルグやコルビエールの詩への傾倒から始まるフランス象徴派詩人達の影響は、詩に客観性を取り戻すというエリオット的課題、彼自身の言葉を借りれば、

> The only way of expressing emotion in the form of art is by finding an 'objective correlative';[3]

という主張と関連して、彼の詩の中でどのような変化を見せているのだろうか。即ち、'vision' と客観性という一見、相入れない要素を詩の中で如何に調和させ、定着させていっているのだろうか。

Helen Gardnerは *The Art of T. S. Eliot* の中で、"Mr Eliot has always been a poet of vision." と述べ、エリオットの詩の基本的な性格を形造っているものとして 'vision' を取り挙げている。そしてさらに、英詩における伝統的な幻想詩人達とは異なって、エリオットの詩の特異性は次の点にあると述べている。

> His unique distinction among English poets is the ballance he has maintained between the claims of his vision and the claims of his art. In his poetry he is neither a prophet nor a visionary primarily, but a poet, a great 'maker'.[4]

つまり、Gardnerはエリオットの詩のスタイルが神秘的であると同時に主知的で技巧的であることをいっているのであって、それは現代における新しい 'visionary poet' としてのエリオットの紹介だと言い換える事が出来る。エリオットの詩における 'vision' とは、詩それ自体による、即ち、詩の構成要素の関係の仕方による詩の創造に基づいている。また、Gardnerはエリオット自身の批評の文章を引用して、彼の詩の展開を、'boredom, terror and glory' という 'vision' の変遷として象徴的に捉えて

いるがエリオットの'vision'の創造は，後に詳しく触れる事になるが,「文芸とは観念を彫琢して表現に仕上げること」だというマラルメの発言を実践しているものとして象徴詩の流れの中で見ることが可能である。

　19世紀以前の詩とは異なって，一般的な意味での'narrator'や'story'の欠如は，エリオットのモダニストとしての最大の特徴である'form'と'feeling'の同一視，思想を感情に置き換えるという芸術的な表現と相俟って彼独自の世界を展開している。主題と表現の新しい在り方をエリオットをはじめ，モダニスト達は模索している。Joyceの作品において革新的なスタイルを作り出す事になった神話の採用や，句読点の省略，文章の継続，大文字の使用の拒否等の新しい表現形態に似て，*Prufrock*の夢や，*The Waste Land*の神話，*Four Quartets*の音楽，といった様々な'form'をエリオットは彼の'vision'の大きなわく組みとしている。1930年の*Baudelaire*の中で，

> ...the care for perfection of form, among some of the romantic poets of the nineteenth century, was an effort to support, or to conceal from view, an inner disorder. Now the true claim of Baudelaire as an artist is not that he found a superficial form. but thathe was searching for a form of life.[5]

と，エリオットは述べているが，皮肉な事にそれは彼自身の詩人としての生涯や芸術についても言えることである。というのはエリオットは*Prufrock*や*The Waste Land*の完成やその経過に必ずしも満足していなかったからである。例えば，これはPoundとの関わりが大きいのだが，*Prufrock*の中の「いや，おれはハムレットじゃない」で始まる数行についてこの一節だけ多分に説明的であり抽象的だとしてPoundに削除を求められたと言われており，また*The Waste Land*のファクシミリーの注には，この詩の中で一時的な生命以上のものをもつ行は，'the 29 lines of water-dripping song of the last part'[6]（最終部の水の歌29行）であると，

エリオットのヴィジョンとサンボリスム

エリオットがこの詩の出版後一年しか経たない1923年に，ある手紙の中で述べている事が記されている。このように博学を駆使して過去の詩の断片を自分の詩に組み込む作詩法を英詩に導入しながらも，'vision'の'maker'としては持続する満足を持ち得ず，エリオットは'form'を求め続ける事になる。これはモダニストとしてのエリオットの苦悩であり，詩を生み出す内的必然性を持ちながら，その表現に関してエリオットがロマン主義の傾向を脱し切れずにいる事を物語っている。そして，彼が*The Waste Land*におけるわずか29行にわたる詩を永遠のものとみなしている理由は，その水の歌が韻律とイメージの完全な一体化を遂げており，主題である魂の枯渇の救済を詩における言葉以外の何ものにも依存しないで表現しているからだと考えられる。詩はその詩句だけで独立した'vision'を伝達する事に成功している点で'vision'の完全な客観的相関物となっており，言葉を生かすための技巧や'form'が主題そのものである新しい詩のスタイルは新しい'vision'の創造を内に含んでいるという事が出来るであろう。

Gardnerは英詩における典型的な'vision'の詩人としてLangland, Vaughan, Traherne, Smart, Blake, Wordsworth等を挙げている。例えば，Langlandの詩には中世キリスト教を背景に'struggle for salvation'（救済への苦闘）がテーマとして存在し，「ヨーロッパ詩人として最大のvisionary poetはDanteである」とGardnerは述べている。Gardnerの幻想詩人に関する論旨には底流としてキリスト教があり，宗教を背景にした英詩の歴史を想い起こさせる。しかし，20世紀初頭の詩人として，エリオットの詩の出発点にあったものは象徴派詩人達，とりわけ，マラルメの純粋詩の作詩法の基本にある「詩は言葉そのものによって書かれるものだ」という，従来の詩へのアンチテーゼであった。宗教性の色濃い'vision'を生み出す後の彼の詩の創作に関して言えば，Danteへの傾倒やDonneやMiltonの詩の評価の変化にも表われているように，詩における技術面よりも信仰や成熟という問題に関心が移っていく事も考慮に入れなければならない。このような変化や'orthodoxy'への到達はGardnerのいう'visionary poets'（幻想詩人達）の系譜にエリオットも連らなるという事に他ならない。

　しかしながら，後期のエリオットの詩の特徴として，さらに音楽の問題が取り挙げられなければならない。改宗以後,直接的に神への帰依をうたった*Ash Wednesday*等の詩と異なって，詩の音楽性に注目し，それを'form'として取り入れている事実は，現代の宗教詩として*Four Quartets*を考える上で重要である。「詩の概念は両極端，即ち，教訓と魔術の間で揺れ動いているようにみえる」とC. M. バウラは彼の著書である『象徴主義の遺産』の中で語っているが,詩における'incantation'の機能が再発見され，また，バラ園におけるような至福の瞬間がうたわれ，哲学的に人間の生に対する究極的な解答が見つけ出されても，さらに詩はうたわれ続けなけれはならないところに現代における宗教詩の役割と，その伝達の難しさがあると言えるであろう。むしろ，そのような詩は懐疑主義を内在させ，そこに逆説的に詩の深まりと成功がある，と言った方がより真実に近いかもしれない。*Four Quartets*の音楽性についてはGardnerによって詳しい分析がされており，[7]四つ強勢の行を基調に，三つあるいは六つの強勢のある行の中で哲学的思索の内容がうたわれているが，教訓にも魔術にも偏る事が出来ず，その間で揺れ続ける詩として*Four Quartets*は1940年代前半の時代思潮を映し出すと同時に，今日なお詩の在り方を問い続けている開かれた詩であると言えるであろう。

　Gardnerはエリオットの詩の展開を'boredom, terror and glory'というエリオットの世界観（vision of the world）の変遷ととらえ，宗教を基盤にした英詩の伝統的な'vision'の観点から解釈している。では,エリオットの詩の出発点にあった象徴派詩人達の求めた'vision'とは何だったのか。それはエリオットの詩の展開の中で究極的に彼の詩と矛盾し，離脱してゆくものだったのか。結論を言えば，象徴詩も，「普通の意識以上の反応を呼び起こす」ための暗示の文学として，'vision'の喚起を目的としていたのである。

　Ronald Bushによると，10代後半のエリオットはマラルメの現実の忘却

の上に成立する超自然にはあまり関心がなかったが，コルビエールの「黄色い恋」[8]やラフォルグの「嘆き節」[9]——前者は欺瞞と裏切りの，後者は恋の成就に足踏みする類の恋の歌——に魅かれ，それらの作品をふまえた多くの習作があると言われている。

　象徴詩の流れには大きく言って，ボードレール→マラルメ→ヴァレリーのいわゆる主流に対して，ややデカダンの臭いのするボードレール→ランボー→ヴェルレーヌの抒情的象徴主義，そしてマラルメ→コルビエール→ラフォルグの支流などがあると言われ，エリオットはラフォルグやコルビエールをイギリスに盛んに紹介し，そのためにその難解なスタイルにもかかわらず，フランス本国よりも英米において先に研究の先鞭がつけられたと言われている。もちろんエリオットの関心はイギリス形而上派詩人達のスタイルとの類似性にあったが，ラフォルグやコルビエールには他の象徴主義の詩人達にはない'wit'や'irony'があった。そして何よりも，より現実的であった。*Prufrock*よりも少し前の1909年に書かれた*Conversation Gallante*はシモンズの*Symbolist Movement*に紹介されていたラフォルグの詩の一つをほぼそっくり模倣したものであるが，その中にみられる'mad poetics'という言葉が示唆するように，後の*Prufrock*や*Portrait*も含めて彼の恋の歌の多くは自己内発的なものではない。繊細で分析好きなラフォルグが月に向かい，またみずからをピエロと任じて恋をうたったり，不具者で反逆者風のコルビエールが執拗にかなえられぬ心を詩にしたのとは違って，エリオットには彼らの詩を相対化し，より客観的に詩を創造する'artisan'としての関心が強かった。

　1905年にすでにエリオットは独自の比喩の世界に遊び，*Morning at the Window*という詩を書いている。

Morning at the Window

They are rattling breakfast plates in basement kitchen,
And along the trampled edges of the street

第一章　T. S. エリオット

I am aware of the damp souls of housemaids
Sprouting despondently at area gates.

The brown waves of fog toss up to me
Twisted faces from the bottom of the street,
And tear from a passer-by with muddy skirts
An aimless smile that hovers in the air
And vanishes along the level of the roofs.[10]

　　　　「窓辺の朝」

彼らは地下の台所で朝食の食器をガラガラやっている。
そして踏み慣らされた通りの両はしに沿って
湿った女中達の魂が地下の勝手口で
元気なく芽を吹いているのに私は気づく。

褐色の霧の波が通りの底から
ねじれた顔を私に投げ上げる，
そして泥だらけのスカートをはいた通行人から
当てもない笑いをもぎとり，それは空にさまよい
そして屋根づたいに消えていく。

ここにはエリオットの生涯のテーマである生の中の死，そして水死のテーマがすでにある。ボードレールの倦怠の世界に似て，こけのように芽を吹く魂や，霧の水底から打ち上げられる通行人の顔，といったイメージやメタファーは超現実主義的であり，主観的なファンタジーの世界を絵画風に構成している。これは一枚の超現実主義の印象風景画であり，詩の背景にいる詩人の存在や思想を考えることの不必要な，詩行だけで成立する独立した詩の世界の出現という点で，モダニストとしてのエリオットの出発点

を示す作品のひとつである。諷刺の効いた，静的な'vision'を呼び起こすこのようなファンタジーの世界をうたった習作の後に，それと非常に性質の似た象徴派の世界との出会いがあった。「パリは私にとって詩そのものであった」と，留学当時をふり返ってエリオットは語っているが，象徴派の詩の世界は一種の非常に個人的で内的な比喩の世界であり，単に従来の比喩の関節をはずしたナンセンスの詩であるにとどまらず，そこには時代を写し出す現実性と超自然があった。

サンボリストに共通する事は，外界を拒否した詩的世界を築くためには，彼らにとって'denotation'（明示：シンボルとオブジェクトが直接に関わる状態）がもはやリアリティーを持たなくなり，新しい明示し難い「魂の状態」を表現するために，それぞれの語が持つ'connotation'（内包：シンボルが対象物の概念にかかわる状態）に依存せざるを得なくなったという事である。Genesias Jonesによれば'words'は本質的にシンボルであり，まれにサインになるという。「示すもの」が「対象物」を直接さし示すのではなく，概念を容れる容器である時，「示すもの」はサインではなくシンボルになっている。象徴派の運動によって一層明らかになった事実の一つがこの，語の機能ということである。象徴派の詩の読者はその超現実主義的傾向と，一見ナンセンスに近い詩風に驚かされるのだが，それはその詩的世界が外的世界における対象物と直接的な関係を絶った「語」（words）の独立を招き，ランボーの「母音の詩」やボードレールの「万物照応」の詩にみられるように，意味の錯乱や感覚の融合という現象を引き起こしているからである。'connotation'に対する象徴派の姿勢はさらに洗練され，より理解しやすいものとして'personal symbols'を生み出している。それらは変形されたメタファーの一種であり，エリオットの言葉で言えば「現代の生活における何か普遍的なもの」を表わしたり，それらを「第一級の'intensity'にまで高める」要素や力がなけれは非常に恣意的な'game'になりやすい性質のものだと言える。ボードレール，マラルメ，コルビエール，ラフォルグから例を挙げてみることにする。

第一章　T. S. エリオット

○ Mon chat sur le carreau cherchant une litière
　Agite sans repos son corps maigre et galeux.[11]
$$\textit{SPLEEN}$$

敷わらを捜す舗道の我が猫は
やせたかいせんの身体を休みなくゆする。
「ゆううつ」　ボードレール

○ Le virge, le vivace et le bel aujourd'hui [12]
$$\textit{PLUSIEURS SONNETS II}$$
処女，快活そして美しい今日という日
「ソネット集　2」マラルメ

○ SOMMEIL! ─ Caméléon tout pailleté d'étoiles!
　Vaisseau-fantôme errant tout seul à pleines voiles![13]
$$\textit{LITANIE DU SOMMEIL}$$

睡眠よ！　星をいっぱい金ぴかに散らしたカメレオン！
ただ独り，満帆全速力でさ迷いゆく幽霊船よ！
「睡眠への連祷」コルビエール

○ Que l'autan, que l'autan
　Effiloche les savates que le temps se tricote![14]
$$\textit{L'HIVER QUI VIENT}$$
南風が，南風が
「時」が毛糸で編んだ上履きを解きほぐしてしまうのだ。
「冬が来る」　ラフォルグ

このように象徴詩は，すべてのものが対応関係にあり，適切な結合の仕方でさえあれば新しい詩の領域，新しい詩の世界を創造することになった。

そしてそれは現代に生きる人間の魂の様態を写し出す事を可能にしているとはいうものの，社会からの逃避的な傾向を逸れない数々のつぶやきであり，幻想であった。

　象徴派の詩に出発点を置きながらエリオットの詩そのものは暗示の文学ではなく，入念に考えられた言葉やイメージの使用による驚きと連想の世界である。*Prufrock*は成就されない恋のうたい方を，分析好きで独自の自由詩の名手であるラフォルグとコルビエールに習い，その心理を'magic lantern'でのぞきこんだ詩である。ここにはエリオットの後の詩に現われる倫理的，宗教的な'vision'はまだない。静止の一点を求めながら，幻想が意識の中を流れ続ける。詩はうたい続けられ，内的ドラマは展開してゆくが，外的には何も起こらず，何も始まらない。意識の流れの手法は象徴派の目差した静的な'vision'の一つの表現形式として発展したものであり，そこで経過する時間は*Ulysees*にも見られるように，小説の長さとは無関係に非常に短かく，可能な限り非時間の世界に近づこうとしている。意識の流れによって創造される世界は日常の時間を越えたところに心理的なリアリズムを築こうとしている。エリオットにとっては，それはプルーフロックのような劇的登場人物の創造に向かう事であり，ペルソナを用いる事であった。そしてさらに，彼は神話の中の登場人物の利用に進んでいく。

　*The Waste Land*は時間的にも空間的にも大規模な連想の織り物といった様子を呈している。そして各断片が織り成す壮大な歴史的展望は生の中の死，再生への力ない願望を感じさせ，そこに作者の思想や宗教観が顔をのぞかせている。Tiresiasは，荒廃した現代の状況を写し出す各断片に統一を与え，みずから愛と欲望の数千年を生きる神話的人物として，この詩を集約し，象徴する人物である。言い変えれば，エリオットの目に写った世界観の化身である。第三部*The Fire Sermon*の中の有名なタイピストの情事の場面で，Tiresiasは伝統的な恋の詩の詩形であるソネットの中に登場している。

> The time is now propitious, as he guesses,
> The meal is ended, she is bored and tired,
> Endeavours to engage her in caresses
> Which still are unreproved, if undesired.
> Flushed and decided, he assaults at once;
> Exploring hands encounter no defence;
> His vanity requires no response,
> And makes a welcome of indifference.
> (And I Tiresias have foresuffered all
> Enacted on this same divan or bed;
> I who have sat by Thebes below the wall
> And walked among the lowest of the dead.)
> Bestows one final patronising kiss,
> And gropes his way, finding the stairs unlit…[15]
>
> *The Waste Land*, 235-248.

この14行は ababcdcdefefgg と韻を踏む典型的なShakespearean sonnetであるが，時間を越えた，しかも，かっこ付きの劇的なTiresiasの登場の仕方は，詩形と内容のずれを一層大きくし，皮肉なデフォルメとなっている。また，かっこ内の4行は*Prufrock*における説明的な部分に似て，この詩の解明になっている。*Ulysees*においてJoyceが現代人と神話の中の登場人物を対照させた方法とは違って，エリオットはTiresiasを導入することによって，現代の荒廃と無秩序，何かの喪失感を導入している。*The Wasted Land*の各断片は一つのテーマを演奏する異なった楽器であり，この詩全体はいわゆる観念の音楽である。神話は生きる事における何か根元的なもの，本質的なものを具体的に，客観的に感得させる一つの 'form' であり，神話の中の様々な登場人物は内在的にある普遍性を持っている。それは*The Wasted Land*の中で，秩序を回復するための芸術的，構造的コントロールの手段として用いられている。しかし，この詩の読者は読み

エリオットのヴィジョンとサンボリスム

進むにつれて，類推によって一つのパターンをくり返し発見していく作業を行っているのに気づき始める。象徴詩の先駆的存在であるE. A. Poeは彼の詩論の中で長編詩を否定し，一篇の詩に一つの'mood'や'emotion'の表現，という在り方を述べているが，ある絶対性または普遍性に近づくために現代においては神話や音楽を用いることによって，長編詩が可能となっているのだ。*The Wasted Land*で読者は，各断片の客観的相関物を通して生・死・再生というパターンを発見し続け，一つの観念に集約し，体験する事によってそれを獲得するのである。そして，この詩における多くの'vision'は単なる幻想ではなくて，読者の追体験の努力の結果喚起される一つの観念のインカネーションとも言えるものになっているのである。

　エリオットは詩における'form'を常に捜し続けている。それは'emotion'から逃げる事であり'feeling'に置き換える事であり，客観的相関物を見出す事であった。さらに詩の大きなわく組みとしては白昼夢や神話も利用している。*The Wasted Land*は読者に生・死・再生のパターンを発見し，魂の枯渇とその救済というテーマに到る過程を追体験させ，それらを再構成させる事を余儀なくする。そのダイナミズムこそエリオット独自の'vision'の創造の仕方である。その手法は，ラフォルグの'dramatic monologue'によって触発され，意識の流れの手法や，神話と現代の状況との類雑によって発展させられてきたものである。エリオットの詩の世界は，*Little Gidding*の中にある語を用いれば'still forming'の世界である点に特色がある。しかし，それはまた象徴主義の詩法の一つでもあり，象徴主義の詩法から言えば'personal symbol'の創造であり，その'symbol'の詩への定着の過程，ダイナミズムにエリオットの詩のおもしろさがあると言える。例えば，

　I have measured out my life with coffee spoons,[16]

の中の「コーヒースプーン」や，より劇的な構成の中の，

I remember
Those are pearls that were his eyes.
'Are you alive, or not? Is there nothing in your head?'[17]

　の中にある'Shakespeherian Rag'と呼ばれる1行のおもしろさである。倦怠や魂の枯渇の'symbol'が，1行の中に，スタンザの変形である断片の中に，そして断片と断片の間の隔絶を越え，統合された詩の全体に拡大され，詩は重層的に現代の生を描き，より普遍的なものに高められていく。詩を構成する単位はより大きな単位へとその役割りを転嫁させていく。その中心にある核は *The Waste Land* に象徴され *Four Quartets* に受け継がれていくある偉大な喪失感である。

　中心の喪失。到達することのないそれに向かって永遠に近づく運動，すなわち詩があるばかりである。*The Waste Land* の最終部分は引用の並列で有名な箇所であり，それぞれの引用の出典も明らかにされているが，それは一種の祈りでもある。

　　　　I sat upon the shore
　　Fishing, with the arid plain behind me
　　Shall I at least set my lands in order?
　　London Bridge is falling down falling down falling down
　　Poi s'ascose nel foco che gli affina
　　Quando fiam uti chelidom-O swallow swallow
　　Le Prince d'aquitaine à la tour abolie
　　These fragments I have shored against my ruins
　　Why then Ile fit you. Hieronymo's mad againe.
　　Datta. Dayadhvam. Damyata,
　　　　Shantih shantih shantih[18]
　　　　　　　　　　　　The Waste Land, 423-433.

それぞれの客観的相関物の理解の後に，また理解を越えたところに詩の伝達の可能性を求めているのであり，詩の喚起（invocation）に重点がある点では象徴派詩人としてのエリオットの姿をあきらかに認めることができる箇所である。この詩の喚起（invocation）の問題は*Four Quartets*の音楽とも関連し，それはまた，純粋詩を求めたマラルメの問題ともそれほど遠くはない。

マラルメにとって詩とは，語そのものによって書かれ，語の前後関係によって暗示され，語をこの世界の塵芥から洗い浄める行為であった。彼にとって「民族の言葉の純化」とは美的，観念的問題だったが，エリオットにとっては倫理的，宗教的問題だった。しかし，エリオットは詩の音楽についてマラルメの理論を踏襲している。マラルメにとって音楽は文芸と同じ目的を持つものであり音楽も文芸も「神秘」を表現する方法であって，「新しい意味での音楽とは，魔法を理解力の場に喚起するもの」，そして「奪い返すべき我々詩人の財産である」と言っている。なぜならマラルメにとって，

> …ce n'est pas de sonorités élémentaires par les cuivres, les cordes, les bois, indéniablement mais de l'intellectuelle parole à son apogée que doit avec plénitude et évidence, résulter, en tant que l'ensemble des rapports existant dans tout, la Musique.[19]
>
> *Crise de Vers,* by Stéphane Mallarmé

音楽が，この宇宙の万物の相関関係を全部表わすという本来の機能を発揮し，その充実した明らかな姿で現われるのは，けっして木管，金管，弦などからでるなまの音響によるのではなく，最高度に達した時の知的な言語の働きによるのだからである。

「詩の危機」ステファヌ・マラルメ

象徴詩を暗示の文学と呼ぶ時の暗示とは，「対象物から引き出される消えやすい移ろいやすい観念のオーラであり，言葉の音楽性である」とマラル

メは述べている。象徴詩における'vision'はこの言葉の音楽性と密接に結びついている。即ち，'vision'は言葉が記憶の中で持続している間においてだけ，その前後関係によって立ち上る光景である。エリオットも「詩の音楽」の中で，言葉が理解出来なくても，詩が人の心を動かすならば，その詩は何かを意味しているのであり，そうでないならばその詩は何も言っていないのだ，とマラルメと同じ趣旨の事を述べている。詩の音韻による魔術的要素'incantation'によって二人は異なる目標に向かってではあるが，失なわれた何か絶対なるものを追求し続けているのである。そして'incantation'そのものが絶対なるものへの過程であり，目的である点について言えば，'form'と'feeling'の同一視を完成しているモダニズムの詩である*The Waste Land*の時期を後にして，*Four Quartets*はポスト・モダニズムの詩の世界に移っていると言えるのである。

*Little Gidding*の'compound ghost'との出会いの場面は'visionary poet'としてのエリオットの頂点にあるものの一つであろう。『神曲』の一場面を模倣したものであり，*Ash Wednesday*で予告されていた'the unread vision in the higher dream'である。しかし，この部分は人類の歴史に刻まれ続けてきた愚行と探究についての冥想詩であり，構成上，五部に分かれ，火，水，土，空気の4つのシンボルを用いながらも，その音楽は形式的で弱々しい。'vision'は思想や宗教から独立した，語そのものによって生まれてくるのではなく，すでに用意されており，詩全体にたくさんのトポスが特別な用い方によって散在している。それはマラルメの言葉であったり*Hamlet*に出てくる状況設定や詩句そのものである。そしてエリオットの世界観，'vision'を最も端的に象徴している語が，

>　The day was breaking. In the *disfigured* street
>　He left me, with a kind of valediction,
>　And faded on the blowing of the horn.[20]（斜字体は筆者のもの）
>　　　　　　　　*Little Gidding* 147-149

エリオットのヴィジョンとサンボリスム

の中の頃 'disfigured' である。それは第一義的には「木の葉が散って汚れた」という意味であるが，人間の存在，生そのものを罪悪視するエリオットの原罪の意識を暴露している。博学を駆使し，自己の苦しみに宗教的，哲学的解決を見つけ出しながらも，あくまでそれらの詩における定着と心の平和を疑わしめる点は*Four Quartets*も*The Waste Land*と変わらないようにみえる。エリオットのスタイルは 'still forming' に象徴され，その意味で終わりはいつも始まりなのである。至福の 'vision' は詩の中に定着する事がない。それは，マラルメが，

> Quelque chose comme les Lettres existe-t-il; Autre (une convention fut, aux époques classiques, cela) que l'affinement, vers leur expression burinée, des notions, en tout domaine.[21]
>
> *La Musique et Les Lettres*

> いったい文芸というものは存在するのか。もし存在するとすればその仕事は，古典の諸時代にそうだったように，社会のあらゆる分野で，観念を彫琢して表現に仕上げることではないのか。
>
> 「音楽と文芸」

という時の「観念」に他ならないからである。エリオットの詩における 'vision' は多くの場合否定的なものであり，エリオットは 'negative visionary' であると言える。至福の 'vision' とはバラ園の子供達の笑い声や*East Coker*の地における古代の人の舞踏等であるが，それらは一種の郷愁であり，現実と遊離した観念への逃避でしかない。そして，それらをうたうことによって逆に至福の 'vision' の遠さを感じさせるのである。

　マラルメの詩法について次第に関心を深めながらも，エリオットは純粋詩について完全には共感を持つ事が出来ないでいた。このことについては改宗という私的な問題が関係してくる事は周知の通りである。Ronald Bushによると1933年のアメリカでの一連のTurnbull Lecturesの中でエ

リオットは,「明喩や暗喩が必ずいつも想像力にはっきり写らなければならないと想定するのは誤りである」と語っている。そして語そのものの重要性とコンテキストへの依存を重視する発言をしており,詩における'incantation'への傾倒をますます強めている。1935年に書かれ,出版された*Burnt Norton*の中で,エリオットはマラルメの詩を踏襲し,静止点を求めながら廻り続けるこの世界（turning world）を,暗示的で形而上学的なイメージとリズムを展開させながら,うたっている。

> Garlic and sapphires in the mud
> Clot the bedded axle-tree.
> The trilling wire in the blood
> Sings below inveterate scars
> Appeasing long forgotten wars.
> The dance along the artery
> The circulation of the lymph
> Are figured in the drift of stars
> Ascend to summer in the tree
> We move above the moving tree
> In light upon the figured leaf
> And hear upon the sodden floor
> Below, the boarhound and the boar
> Pursue their pattern as before
> But reconciled among the stars.[22]
>   *Burnt Norton* 49-63.

泥まみれのニンニクとサファイアが
埋まった車軸にべたついている。
血液のわななく鉄線が
ぬぐい難い傷痕の皮下で歌って

亡却の底にある戦争を慰撫する。
動脈を行く舞踏
リンパ液の循環は
運行する星々に象られ
木を昇って夏を作る
ぼくらは模様のある葉にそそぐ光となって
ゆれ動く木の上方に移動し
目の下の，湿った地上に
狩る犬と狩られる猪が
むかしのままの図式の追跡をつづけながら
星の座の中では和解しているのを見る。

　　　　　　　　（二宮尊道　訳）

　象徴詩の模倣から始まり，その主観的で閉じられた'vision'をより客観的な理解の場に戻し，そして最後に，祈りや'incantation'へと発展させられた詩へとエリオットは進んでいる。祈りや音楽といった'invocation'（喚起）を考慮した詩に到達しているという意味において，エリオットは象徴詩に再び帰っているということができるのである。
　'vision'は空想や幻想，展望など多くの分野で様々な意味で使われるが，エリオットの詩においては世界観を示す言葉でもある。そして，それはエリオットの詩の本質に関わっており，彼の詩の変遷の中で，モダニストとしての芸術の在り方に深く結びついている。それは20世紀初頭の都市に生きた人間の心理的リアリズムの創造であり，サンボリスムの比喩の世界に生じる'invocation'（喚起）という一種独特の静と動の詩の創作方法を展開させる。エリオットと'vision'の関係についてさらにつけ加えるならば，The Waste Land創作の後もポストモダニストとしてのエリオットの詩の中には一貫して象徴主義の基本的な創作の姿勢が消えることはないのである。そして，最終的に現実への足場をはずし，観念の世界を出る事がなかったという点では，純粋詩，宗教詩の範疇を別にすれば，エリオットの詩の

旅の終わりはマラルメの閉じられた世界への帰還と言うことができると思われる。

注
1) Davie, Donald. *The End of An Era*, (Macmillan, 1956, Casebook) 155.
2) Eliot, T. S. *Collected Poems 1909-1962*, (Faber & Faber, 1970), 205.
3) Eliot, T. S. *Selected Essays*, (Faber & Faber, 1972), 145.
4) Gardner, Helen. *The Art of T. S. Eliot*, (Faber & Faber, 1972), 185.
5) Eliot, *Selected Essays*, 424.
6) Eliot, T. S. *The Waste Land: A Facsimile & Transcript of The Original Drafts*, (Faber & Faber, 1971), 129.
7) cf. Gardner, *The Art of T. S. Eliot*, 29-33.
　　Tíme présent and tíme pást
　　Are bóth perhaps présent in tíme fúture,
　　And tíme fúture contáined in tíme past.
　　Dówn the pássage which we díd not táke
　　Towards the dóor we néver ópened.
　　・・・
　　The détail of the páttern is móvement,
　　Ás in the figure of the tén stáirs.
　　Desíre itsélf is móvement
　　Nót in itsélf desírable;
　　Lóve is itsélf unmóving,
　　Ónly the cáuse and énd of móvement,
　　・・・
　　At the stíll póint of the túrning wórld. Neither flésh nor fléshless ;
　　Neither fróm nor towárds; at the stíll póint, thére the dánce is,
　　But néither arrést nor movement.　And dó not cáll it fíxity,
8) cf. 加藤美雄『フランス象徴詩研究』(駿河台出版社, 1979), 89-90.
　　Sentir sur ma lèvre appauvrie
　　Ton dernier baiser se gercer,
　　La mort dans tes bras me bercer...
　　Me déshabiller de la vie!
　　　　　　　　　　Un jeune Qui S'en Va,
　　　　　　　　　　dernière strophe

エリオットのヴィジョンとサンボリスム

by Tristan Corbiere.

血の気をなくした僕の唇の上で
お前の最後の接吻がひび割れるのを感じる。
死がお前の腕の中で僕をゆすぶり…
僕から生命という服を脱がせるのがわかる。
「立ち去る者」
最終節
トリスタン・コルビエール

9) Laforgue, Jules. *Poesies completes,* (Editions Gallimard et Librairie, 1970), 85.

Celle qui doit me mettre au courrant de la Femme!
Nous lui dirons d'abord, de mon air le moins froid:
"La somme des angles d'un triangle, chère âme,
 "Est égale a deux droit."

Et si ce cri lui part: "Dieu de Dieu: que je t'aime!"
 — "Dieu reconnaîtra les siens. Ou piquée au vif :
 — "Mes claviers ont du coeur, tu seras mon seul thème."
 Moi: — "Tout est relatif."

Aulre Complainte de Lord Pierrot,
premières deux strophes
by Jules Laforgue.

僕をいっぱしのおんなつうにしてくれるはずの女よ,
わたくしはまず言うのだ, 一番つめたいそぶりで,
「三角形の内角の和は, 愛する人よ,
 二直角に等しい。」

そして, もし彼女が「ああもう, わたしはあなたをこんなに愛している」と叫ぶなら
 ——「神様は身内の者だとお認め下さるだろう。」それがしゃくにさわって,
 ——「わたしの鍵盤には心があるの, あなたがわたしのたった一つの主題なの。」
  僕,「すべては相対的だ。」

「ピエロ卿のもう一つの嘆き」
最初の二節，
ジュール・ラフォルグ

10) Eliot, *Collected Poems 1909-1962*, 29.
11) Baudelaire, Charles. *Les Fleurs du Mal,* Editions Garnier Fréres, 1961, 78.
12) Mallarmé, Stéphane Œuvres Complétes, Gallimard, 1945, 67.
13) cf. 加藤美雄『フランス象徴詩研究』,『フランス文学講座5・詩』大修館書店, 260.
14) cf. Laforgue, Jules. *Poesies completes,* 281.
15) Eliot, *Collected Poems 1909-1962*, 72.
16) Eliot, *Collected Poems 1909-1962*, 14.
17) Eliot, *Collected Poems 1909-1962*, 67.
18) Eliot, *Collected Poems 1909-1962*, 79.
19) Mallarmé, Stéphane. *Œuvres Complétes,* 367-368.
20) Eliot, *Collected Poems 1909-1962*, 219.
21) Mallarmé, Stéphane. *Œuvres Complètes,* 645.
22) Eliot, *Collected Poems 1909-1962*, 190-191.

詩形のエチュード

――エリオットのフランス詩とフォーム――

　T.S.エリオットがみずからを文学における古典主義者と称し，宣言してから半世紀以上が過ぎた。しかし，50年代以降，ロマン主義と現代との連続性を見ようとする批評活動が盛んになるにつれて，エリオットの文学活動におけるロマン主義の傾向を指摘し，個性の滅却を唱えたエリオット自身を，皮肉にも，ロマン派の流れの中に位置づけ，今日までの20世紀の文学運動を概ね，ロマン主義の継続とみる見方が主流になってきた。エリオットの反ロマン主義はロマン派の詩人たちの個性の放縦，啓蒙という名のもとにプロパガンダに陥ってしまった詩に対する危機感，普遍性という古典主義の理想と基盤の喪失，等にあったわけだが，今日，エリオットもまた20世紀における大きな一つの個性として位置づけられようとしている。小論はこのような観点をふまえながら，いわゆる古典主義者エリオットが初期の頃に書いたフランス語による四つの詩の中にエリオットのロマン主義的特徴がどのように表れているのか，主としてサンボリストとの関係から考察しようとしたものである。

1．詩形のエチュード

　　感動の詩につくべきか，それとも「動機のない」詩，純粋に美学的な詩につくべきか？ボードレールの天才，その成功は，これら二つの選択のうちどちらかひとつをほかのひとつのために切り捨てることではないだろう。それぞれのゆきすぎを慎重に測り，言語と形式が感動に対して，そしてもっと一般的に霊感（インスピレーション）に対して

第一章　T. S. エリオット

もつ関係がそれ自体あらたな関係になるような新しい道を，提示することにあるだろう。[1]

ドミニック・ランセ

　エリオットの詩人としての出発点のひとつに象徴主義の詩の模倣があったことは周知の通りであるが，その後，編集や批評の仕事に携わった時期においても，エリオットは積極的にフランスのサンボリストたちを紹介している。そしてフランスのサンボリストたちは，一時，イギリスやアメリカの詩人たちの尊敬のまととなった。とりわけ，エリオットによるコルビエールの発見が他の詩人や批評家を刺激したことは有名である。[2]

　しかしながら，1930年にボードレール論が発表されて以後もエリオットのコルビエール研究は出版されなかった。それは，コルビエールや，パウンドに教示されたといわれるゴーチェに対するエリオットの評価の問題に関係してくるように思われる。本格的なサンボリスム研究を発表する以前に，エリオットには改宗という転機が訪れていること，ボードレール論は現代人の救済の問題や宗教的視点から結論づけられていることから，芸術に対する信条と宗教的信条について確固たる拠り所を求めずにはいられなかった伝記的な事実も，エリオットのサンボリスト評価の考慮にいれなければならないだろう。そしてさらに，エリオットの詩そのものにおける象徴主義の資質の存続の有無もエリオットの詩の全体像を考える上で重要になってくるように思われる。

　エリオットのサンボリストたちに対する関心は1908年，20歳の時に，アーサー・シモンズの『文学における象徴主義運動』を読んだことに始まり，彼らに対する意欲的な研究は1910年から1年間，彼がソルボンヌ大学に留学したときに生れたと一般に考えられている。*The Love Song of J. Alfred Prufrock*はこの時期に，パリとミュンヘンで書かれたものであり，有名な書き出しである次の3行，

　　Let us go then, you and I,

> When the evening is spread out against the sky
> Like a patient etherised upon a table; [3]

の中の夕暮のイメージは「手術台の上の傘とミシンの出会い」といったサンボリストのコンシートをエリオットが読んでいたことを想わせる。また、黄色い霧の着想も、彼が『黄色い恋』の詩人、コルビエールを愛好していたことを物語っている。サンボリストへの傾倒が始まったのは1914年のロンドンでのパウンドとの出会いよりもはるか前のことで、エリオットの気質に合い、詩作や詩論の形成の基盤として常に底流としてあったものと思われる。それは、Donald Davieが指摘するように、次のような行からも読み取ることができる。

> But where is the penny world I bought
> To eat with Pipit behind the screen?
>   *A Cooking Egg* (1919)

> The problem once solved, the brown god is almost forgotten
> By the dwellers in cities –
>   ・・・
> His rhythm was present in the nursery bedroom,
> In the rank ailanthus of the April dooryard,
>   *The Dry Salvages* (1941)

Davieはエリオットをサンボリストの伝統のなかに置いてみる見方を継続している批評家の一人だが、「プルーフロックの恋歌」から、「料理用の卵」を含む『1920年詩集』を経て、『四つの四重奏』にいたるまで、エリオットの詩法に一貫してサンボリストの要素が色濃く存在することを指摘しているのは適切だと思われる。Davieはエリオットの詩のサンボリスト的側面について早い時期から次のように述べている。

第一章　T. S. エリオット

'His rhythm was present in…' represents just that bridgework, that filling in and faking of transitions, which Eliot as a post-symbolist poet has always contrived to do without. From first to last his procedure has been the symbolist procedure of 'juxtaposition without coupula', the setting down of images side by side with a space between them, a space that does not need to be bridged.[4]

繋辞なしの並列という手法こそ，サンボリストたちが目指した「普通の意識以上のものを呼び起こす」一つの重要な方法であり，語と語，行と行の相互浸透から生まれてくる静かなセンセーションや詩句の効果の一過性というサンボリスムの特徴を誕生させるものである。しかしながら，サンボリストたちのいう普通の意識以上のものは論理的な陳述によって生まれるのではなく，いわゆる感性の論理ともいうべきものに依存しており，そのため詩人一人一人の個性や恣意的な面が強調されるようになり，難解になってくる。このサンボリスムの芸術としての存亡にかかわるひとつの危機的側面，それはロマン主義芸術の末裔としての一面をサンボリスムがもっていたからに他ならないのであるが，そのことにエリオットは早くから気づいていた。それは詩に客観性を取り戻すというエリオット的課題，彼自身のことばを借りれば，

The only way of expressing emotion in the form of art is by finding an 'objective correlative'[5]

の一文で表されている。「ハムレット論」の中でこのような定義がなされたのは1919年のことである。しかし，彼自身の作品の中にその実践を求めることはまた別の問題とされなければならない。その数年後の『荒地』のファクシミリーの注には，この詩の中で一時的な生命以上のものをもつ行は最終部の水音の歌29行であると，ある手紙の中でエリオットが述べて

詩形のエチュード

いることが記されている。'emptied form' というDavieのエリオットの詩に対する批判は，エリオットの彼自身の詩にたいする満足如何にかかわらず，エリオットの詩に一貫して見られる一つの重要な特徴を言いあてていると言える。サンボリストの二大巨匠，ランボーとマラルメは1891年と1898年にそれぞれ亡くなっている。では，「美」の世紀といわれた19世紀から「生」の世紀である20世紀に入って，サンボリスムの限界を知りながら，エリオットはそれから何を学び，何に執着していったのであろう。

2. 四つのフランス詩

エリオットの詩集には，セレクションにもコレクションにも，フランス語で書かれた四つの詩が掲載されている。とりたてて優れた詩であるといった評価をもつものではないが，1916年から17年にかけて書かれたこれらの詩には習作の時期の様々な試みと，エリオットの詩の特徴がいくつか見いだされる。まず，「ディレクター」という詩を取り上げてみよう。

Le Directeur	「ディレクター」
Malheur à la malheureuse Tamise	スペクテイター社のすぐそばを流れる
Qui coule si près du Spectateur.	哀れなテームズ河に災いあれ。
Le directeur	スペクテイター社の
Conservateur	保守的な
Du Spectateur	ディレクターは
Empeste la brise.	微風を汚している。
Les actionnaires	保守的な
Réactionaires	スペクテイター社の
Du Spectateur	反動的な
Conservateur	株主たちは
Bras dessus bras dessous	腕を組みあい

Font des tours	忍び足で
A pas de loup.	歩きまわる。
Dans un égout	下水の中で
Une petite fille	ぼろを着た
En guenilles	しし鼻の
Camarde	少女が
Regarde	保守的な
Le directeur	スペクテイター社の
Du Spectateur	ディレクターを
Conservateur	ながめては
Et crève d'amour.	恋こがれる。[6]

　何よりも前に，詩形の大胆さに驚かされる。非常に短い行の構成とくり返しは，詩はたった一つのエモーションを表わすものだ，といったE. A. ポーの詩作の方法や，「普通の意識以上のものを呼び起こす」サンボリスムの手法を想わせるものであるが，一種類の脚韻（この詩においてはわずかに不完全であるが）を連続して用いることは英詩では珍しく，その面白さをサンボリストの一人，トリスタン・コルビエール（1845-1875）の詩に学んでいる。早世したこの「押韻家としてもまた詩学者としても，完全無欠なところがまるでない」大詩人は，アンドレ・ブルトンによって，「言語のオートマチスム（自動的展開）がフランス詩にはいりこむのは，おそらく彼の『黄色い恋』からだ」と評されているフランス詩の歴史においても異色の，しかも重要な詩人である。[7]「ディレクター」は皮肉な響きを残しながらゆるやかに流れる音のおもしろさをもっているが，詩の内容は一つのロンドンの社会風景であり，それがシニカルにうたわれている。次のソネ（ソネット）はエリオットが詩作の際に愛の告白の仕方を学んだジュール・ラフォルグのものであるが，詩の内容ばかりでなく詩のフォームを考える上でも当時のエリオットに影響を与えたに違いない。

詩形のエチュード

  Complainte-Épitaphe   「なげきぶし風の墓碑銘」

  La Femme   女というもの
  Mon âme :   俺の魂よ,
  Ah! quels   ああ！何という
  Appels!   呼びかけだ！

  Pastels   命はかない
  Mortels,   パステル画さ,
  Qu'on blâme   色が悪けりゃ
  Meg gammes!   けなすがいいさ！

  Un fou   阿呆一人
  S'avance   進み出て
  Et danse.   道化の踊り。

  Silence...   しーっ...
  Lui, où?   奴だぞ，どこに？
  Coucou.   ほととぎすが鳴いている。[8]
  (*Les Complaintes*, 1885)   （『なげきぶし』 1885）

2音節詩句による正韻ソネの形がとられている。極めて短く，韻律もわずかに一つという行の構成と整った14行の詩形は，恋愛詩でありながら，叙情詩の辺境にあって皮肉な緊張感を伝えている。ラフォルグは空想の恋人に向けてその不義を極端な詩形のなかで嘆いてみせる。このように仮面をつけておどけてみせる主人公の心理はプルーフロックの狐疑逡巡に再現され，凌辱と生の不毛についての嘆きは究極的に『荒地』の水音の歌となって継承されていくのである。次の「あらゆるものの不義なる混合」もコルビエールを模倣したものであり，[9] イメージの中にはランボーを想わせる

第一章　T. S. エリオット

ものもある。

 Mélange Adultère de Tout　　　　　　「あらゆるものの不義なる混合」

 En Amerique, professeur;　　　　　アメリカでは教授,
 En Angleterre, journaliste;　　　　イギリスではジャーナリスト,
 C'est à grands pas et en sueur　　 大股で歩き,汗をかいても
 Qua vous suivrez à peine ma piste.　わたしの後をつけられまい。
 En Yorkshire, conférencier;　　　　ヨークシャーでは講演者,
 A Londres, un peu banquier,　　　　ロンドンではちょっぴり銀行家,
 Vous me paierez bien la tête.　　　君たちは僕のことで頭をひねるのさ。
 C'est à Paris que je me coiffe　　　パリだからこそ僕は冠る
 Casque noir de j emenfoutiste.　　　細事に無関心の黒かぶとを。
 En Allemagne, philosophe　　　　　　ドイツでは,哲学者
 Surexcité par Emporheben　　　　　　昂然として意気上がり
 Au grand air de Bergsteigleben　　　登山生活を我がもの顔,
 J'erre toujours de-ci de-là　　　　　僕はいつもあちこちとさまよい歩く
 A divers coups de tra là là　　　　　トラララのいろんな拍子に合わせて
 De Damas jusqu' à Omaha.　　　　　　ダマスカスからオマハまで。
 Je célébrai mon jour de fete　　　　僕は誕生日を祝うだろう
 Dans une oasis d'Afrique　　　　　　アフリカのオアシスで
 Vêtu d'une peau de girafe.　　　　　キリンの皮を着て。

 On montrera mon cénotaphe　　　　　僕の骨なき記念碑は
 Aux côtes brûlantes de Mozambique.　モザンビックの灼熱の浜に立つだろう。

様々に仮面をつけて自分を紹介する方法は,コルビエールの「コルビエールの墓碑銘」から取られている。後年の『荒地』の構成方法や内容とはまだかなりの隔たりは感じられるものの,一種のカタログのフォームを持ち,

詩形のエチュード

『荒地』のコラージュを連想させる。それらは情緒を芸術の形で表現する方法としてエリオットが関心をもったものであった。[10]

言語と詩句についてのあらゆる技術を知っていたといわれるコルビエールから大きな衝撃と影響をうけたエリオットは、さらにモック・ヘロイックな調子をつけ加え、「君たちは僕のことで頭をひねるのさ」とはまさにエリオットの詩に面食らう読者に対する揶揄である。そして『荒地』に引用されたボードレールの一節と奇しくも符号している。フランス語で書かれた上の二つの詩について言えることは、それらの〈詩の形〉が何よりもまず、重要な意味を持っているということである。さらに、次の二つのフランス語の詩を見てみよう。

Lune de Miel

Ils ont vu les Pays-Bas, ils rentrent à Terre Haute;
Mais une nuit d'été, les voici à Ravenne,
A l'aise entre deux draps, chez deux centraines de punaises;
La sueur aestivale, et une forte odeur de chienne.
Ils restent sur le dos écartant les genoux
De quatre jambes molles tout gonflées de morsures.
On relève le drap pour mieux égratigner.
Moins d'une lieue d'ici est Saint Apollinaire
En Classe, basilique connue des amateurs
De chapitaux d'acanthe que tournoie le vent.

Ils vont prendre le train de huit heures
Prolonger leurs misères de Padoue à Milan
Où se trouve la Cène, et un restaurant pas cher.
Lui pense aux pourboires, et rédige son bilan.
Ils aurant vu la Suisse et traversé la France.
Et Saint Apollinaire, raide et ascétique,

第一章　T. S. エリオット

Vieille usine désaffectée de Dieu, tient encore
Dans ses pierres écroulantes la forme précise de Byzance.

　　「蜜月」
彼らは「低き国」オランダを見物し,「高き地」テル・オートに戻る。
けれど，ある夏の夜，ここ，ラヴェンナにふたり,
くつろぐ二枚のシーツの間，二百匹も南京虫のいるところ,
夏の汗，それに雌犬のひどい匂い。
膝を広げたまま，仰向けにねる,
やわらかな足は四本とも咬み傷で腫れぼったい。
掻きやすいようにシーツをまくりあげる。
ここから一里足らずのところにサンタポリナーレ・アン・クラッセがある,
好事家たちにその名を知られたバシリカだ,
風に舞うアカンサスの柱頭がある。

これから八時間汽車に乗る
パドヴァからミラノまで，このみじめさをひきのばすため
そこには「最後の晩餐」と高くないレストランがある。
男はチップのことを考え，支払いの見積もりをする。
スイスを見，フランスを横断したとして。
さて，冷厳で禁欲のサンタポリナーレ寺院は
用途を変更された神さまの古い工場だが,
崩れ落ちる石のなか，今なお，ビザンチウムの正確な様式を保っている。

新婚歳行の描写の中に聖と俗，精神と肉体が対照させられている。皮肉とユーモアの調子は残忍とも言えるほど押しすすめられている。Grover Smithによると,「蜜月」と次の詩「レストランにて」において，エリオットは自由詩を発展させ，前者では，アレキサンドラン（弱強六歩格）を試みている。ことば遊びや詩語にはコルビエールのものが踏襲されているが,

69

詩形のエチュード

　ここでは、詩形の点からその効果を見てみよう。一行のシラブルの数は主に12であり、セジューラ（行中の休止）がほぼ規則正しく中央に置かれ、物語詩の流れるような調子をつくりだしている。フランス詩におけるアレキサンドランの歴史は古く、次のように定義されている。

> The alexandrine has been, since the 16 century, the standard meter of French poetry, in which it has had an importance comparable to that of the quantative hexameter in Latin poetry or blank verse in English poetry; it has been used especially in dramatic and narrative forms.[11]

　アレキサンドランは12音節詩句で、古代、あるいは中世における8音節や10音節詩句によって書かれた叙事詩に代わって、より叙情的な表現方法として定着していった詩形である。19世紀のサンボリストたちにとって古典的ともいえるこの詩法は、あらゆる詩は音楽であり、軽みでなければならぬ、といったヴェルレーヌの宣言とともに、半句の切れ目の単調さを破ったり、アンジャンブマン（句またぎ）を導入することによって現代の自由詩への道を開いていった。しかしながら、ちょうどこの時期に書かれた *Reflection on Vers Libre*「自由詩について」(1917) の中でエリオットは、この誤解を招きやすい語句について、また、20世紀初頭の文学の無秩序、および自由詩の賛美の傾向に対して、芸術が必然的に形式を要求することを述べている。

> *Vers libre* has not even the excuse of a polemic; it is a battle-cry of freedom, and there is no freedom in art. And as the so-called *vers libre* which is good is anything but 'free'...
> ・・・
> If *vers libre* is a genuine verse-form it will have a positive definition. And I can define it only in negatives: (1) absence of pattern, (2)

absence of rhyme, (3) absence of metre.[12]

　エリオットは韻律や脚韻の必要からの自由があるのではなく，詩の効果のために，それらを自由に駆使する自由があるのだと述べ，自由詩というものは存在せず，良い詩と悪い詩，そして混沌があるのみだと結んでいる。さらに言えば，詩は芸術（の一つの形式）であるかぎり，拘束と原則をもたないという意味で，逆説的に，自由ではありえないのである。フォームについての関心は継続され，1930年の「ボードレール論」における次のような批評文にも見ることができる，

> ...the care for perfection of form, among some of the romantic poets of the nineteenth century, was an effort to support, or to conceal from view, an inner disorder. Now the true claim of Baudelaire as an artist is not that he found a superficial form, but that he was searching for a form of life.[13]

ボードレールは気質からするとロマン主義者であるのに，印象や苦悩や心の底からの情熱が「自然」にはいりこんでくるような，単なる叙情的叙述というものを拒否する。ランセによれば憂鬱と理想，悪徳と美徳，悪魔主義と神秘主義，うす汚れたパリと香り高い島々，日常生活の凡庸と賞揚される死，このように引き裂かれる感受性の激しさと向かいあいながら，それらを容れる器として彼がとった表現手段は8音節詩句，10音節詩句，12音節詩句（アレキサンドラン），さらには14行詩の古い詩形（ソネット）といった「伝統的な古典の詩形」であった。ボードレールは詩的散文，散文詩の領域にも新しい詩的空間を創ることを夢みていたが，その実現は後のランボーを待たなければならない。ボードレールの独創性は散文詩にあるのでも，象徴の使用にあるのでもなく，想像力の新しい用い方，詩的イメージの全体系の提示にあった。周知のように，「万物照応」における感情や感覚や官能の複雑な響き合いは自然の中に潜む万物の普遍的類縁関係を感

得させるものであり，ボードレールにとって完全で無欠な詩とはその神秘的な関係の完全で誤りのない翻訳のことであった。[14] 古典の詩形を踏襲しながらボードレールの超現実的世界は彼独自の美の世界であり，彼を現実から救済するものであった。彼にとって詩形は出発点であり，媒体であり，超現実そのものであった。

　エリオット自身の自由詩についての信条や，彼が大きな影響を受けたサンボリスムの詩人たちの詩から言えることは，エリオットのいう「ロマン派の詩人たちが抱えていた内的無秩序をささえるためのフォーム」の発見という課題がエリオット自身の課題でもあったのではないかということである。ロマン派の叙情的に理想をうたい啓蒙することからさらに進んで，サンボリストたちは古典的なフォームを見直し，かつ，個性的な形而上的詩の世界へとそれを昇華させた。20代のエリオットは彼らの詩のフォームの中に，個人的にしろ社会的にしろ，詩人たちの苦悩や内的混沌をいちはやく察知したに違いない。それは詩人としての出発点にいたエリオットにとって多くの共感をよんだものだった。そして，ボードレールの場合，フォームは詩の文体（スタイル）の内に一体となっている。いや，詩形と内容が切り離されて考えられるべきものでないとすれば，フォームはスタイルそのものなのだ。五感によって伝えられたものを最大限に利用することによって，彼は人間存在の心の深部と肉体の深部に結ばれるすべてのひそやかな調和と連係とを暗示することに成功し，現実が内包している本質的な言葉，「超越性と絶対としての現実」というものを探り当てたのである。言い換えれば，自然は〈象徴〉なるものによって覆い隠された絶対の世界を詩人によって探険され，解読されるのを待っていたのである。

Correspondances

La nature est un temple où de vivants piliers
Laissent parfois sortir de confuses paroles;
L'homme y passe à travers des forêts de symbols

第一章　T.S.エリオット

Qui l'observent avec des regards familiers.

Comme de longs échos qui de loin se confondent
Dans une ténébreuse et profonde unité,
Vaste comme la nuit et comme la clarité,
Les parfums, les couleurs et les sons se réspondent.

Il est des parfums frais comme des chairs d'enfants,
Doux comme les hautbois, verts comme les prairies,
－Et d'autres, corrompus, riches et triomphants,

Ayant l'expansion des choses infinies,
Comme l'ambre, le musc, le benjoin et　1 'encens,
Qui chantent les transports de l'esprit et des sens.[15]

　「万物照応」

〈自然〉は一つの神殿，その生命ある柱は，
ときおり，捉えにくい言葉をかたり，
その中を行く人，象徴の森に分け入る
森の親しげな眼差しに送られながら。

長いこだまが遠くから溶けあうよう
闇の深い合一のうちに，
夜のように光のようにはてもなく，
香りと色と音が合い応える。

ある香り，こどもの肌のようにさわやかで，
オーボエのようにやさしく，牧場のように緑，

——またある香り，腐敗し，豊かに，勝ちほこる，

　　無限のものとおなじひろがりをもって，
　　龍ぜん，麝香，安息香，薫香のように，
　　精神と感覚との熱狂をかなでる。[16]

　前半の8行（オクターブ）はabbacddc，後半の6行（セステット）はefefggと韻を踏み，従来のイタリア風ソネットやペトラルカ風ソネットとは押韻を異にし，最後のカプレットは彼の超現実的，詩的絶対の世界を要約している。ルネッサンス以来低調であったソネットを復活させたのは，ボードレールが『悪の華』を献じたロマン主義者テオフィル・ゴーチェと，上記のような詩を書いたボードレールその人だった。作品がそこに根ざしたとされる生との対決においてすべての意味を獲得するようなそうした作品がボードレールの作品だとするならば，理想と憂鬱の相剋のドラマを古典のフォームでうたうことによってボードレールの作品は単なる現実逃避と嘆きの世界から免れ，彼は彼の求める新たな美の世界を創造することができたのである。ボードレールにとってそれは，エリオットのいう"the care for perfection of form"の成果であり，彼のみが創造しえた'form of life'であった。
　ボードレールが一つの詩的絶対の境地を切り開いたのと違って，エリオットは絶えず満足のゆく詩の世界を模索し，挑戦しなければならなかった。それは最後の詩集である『四つの四重奏』の*Little Gidding*における'still forming'という自分の詩に対する言葉からも察することができる。サンボリストたちのある意味で非常に個性的な詩のスタイルに魅かれながら，それらをお手本にした習作時代のエリオットのフランス語で書かれた詩は，風刺やアイロニーによって直接的な胸中の吐露は避けているにしろ，嘆きや不満にみち，それらを超越して独自の詩的絶対的空間を開拓するまでには至っていない。
　「蜜月」もそうした作品の一つであるが，アレキサンドランという，よ

り叙情的な詩形を用いて同時代の社会風俗を写しだし，風刺している点が興味深い。また，第一，第二スタンザをそれぞれを締め括るかのように，風景の中で神や宗教への言及がなされているが，後のエリオットのキリスト教的世界への傾倒を考えると興味深い。

3．しなやかでしかもぎくしゃくとした詩

　フランス語で書かれた四番めの詩である「レストランにて」は自由詩で書かれ，会話を取り入れたドラマの状況設定と，それから飛躍し，連想されるある叙述の部分から成りたっている。

Dams le Restaurant
Le garcon délabré qui n'a rien à faire
Que de se gratter les doigts et se pencher sur mom épaule:
　'Dans mon pays il fera temps pluvieux,
　Du vent, du grand soleil, et de la pluie;
　C'est ce qu'on appelle le jour de lessive des gueux.'
(Bavard, baveux, à la croupe arrondie,
Je te prie, au moins, ne bave pas dans la soupe).
　'Les saules trempés, et des bourgeons sur les ronces ‒
　C'est là, dans une averse, qu'on s'abrite.
J'avais sept ans, elle était plus petite.
　Elle était tpoute mouillée, je lui ai donné des primeveres.'
Les taches de son gilet montent au chiffre de trente-huit.
　'Je la chatouillais, pour la faire rire.
　J'éprouvais un instant de puissance et de délire.'

　Mais alors, vieux lubrique, â cet age...
'Monsieur, le fait est dur.

詩形のエチュード

　　　Il est venu, nous peloter, un gros chien ;
　　　Moi j'avais peur, je l'ai quittée à mi-chemin.
　　　C'est dammage.'
　　　Mais alor, tu as ton vautour!
　Va t'en te décrotter les rides du visage;
　Tiens, ma fourchette, décrasse-toi le crâne.
　De quell droit payes-tu des expériences comme moi?
　Tiens, voilà dix sous, pour la salle-de-bains.

　Phlébas, le Phlénicien, pendent quinze jours noyé,
　Oubliait les cris des mouette et la houle de Cornouaille,
　Et les profits et les pertes, et la cargaison d'étain
　Un courant de sous-mer l'emporta très loin,
　Le repassant aux étapes de sa vie antérieure.
　Figurez-vous donc, c'etait un sort pénible;
　Cependant, ce fut jadis un bel homme, de haute taille.

　　　「レストランにて」
　みすぼらしい給仕はなにもすることがなくて
　指をこすり合わせ，僕の肩ごしにのぞきこむ。
　　「故郷では，湿っぽい時期がありまして，
　　風がふいたり，かんかん照りだったり，雨がふったりするんです。
　　それを乞食の洗濯日っていうんですよ。」
　（おしゃべり，よだれっくり，でっちりめ，
　お願いだから，せめて，スープの中によだれをたらさないでくれ。）
　　「濡れた柳や，きいちごの芽──
　　夕立にあうと避難するんです，あそこに。
　わたしが七つのときでした，あの子はもっと下でした。
　　あの子はずぶぬれ，わたしは桜草をあげました。」

第一章　T.S.エリオット

この男のチョッキのしみときたら三十八もある。
　「あの子をくすぐってやったんです，笑わせるためにね。
　わたしはちょっとの間えらくなった気がして有頂天でした。」

　ところが，この鄙猥なじいさん，あの歳で…
「だんな，あれはつらかった。
　やって来たんです，すりよって，でっかい犬が。
　わたしは恐くなって，途中でその子を置いてきちゃった。
　残念なことをしました。」
　　で，君も君なりに悔しがっているわけだ。
その皺だらけの顔を洗ってきたまえ。
そら，ガニマタ君，頭の垢を落としておいで。
どうしてまた，僕のように昔語りをしてしまうんだ。
そら，10スーだ，風呂に入っておいで。

フレバスはフェニキア人で，十五日間も溺れたまま，
かもめの泣き声もコルヌアーユの波のうねりも忘れてしまった，
損も得も，錫の船荷のことも。
海底の潮流ははるかに彼を運び，
前世の岸までつれていった。
想像してもみたまえ，ひどい運命もあったものだ，
でも，昔はこれも背の高いいい男だったんだよ。

最後の7行は『荒地』の第四部に改訂され，（このときは英語で）使われたスタンザであり，有名な箇所であるが，この詩でもまず考えさせられるのは，詩のフォームと構成の仕方である。第一，第二スタンザは会話を中心に詩劇仕立てになっており，ドラマへの関心がうかがえる。単に叙情を吐露することを避け，最終的にドラマに向かうエリオットの方向をこのフランス語の詩においても見ることができる。主人公の内的告白が大きな枠組

みとなっている点は「プルーフロックの恋歌」をおもいださせるが、主人公はひそかに語りの役をつとめ、老給仕なる人物の鄙猥な思い出が場末のレストランで展開される。第三スタンザでは、語りは一層、叙述的な調子を帯びてくる。昔語りの老給仕は、風呂ならぬ大洋漂うフェニキア人フレバスの死体となる。このいわゆるフレバス挿話は『荒地』のエリオットの自注にもあるように文化人類学の知識によるものだが、この挿話のみで『荒地』の第四部を構成することになる。その場合は、非常に象徴的に水死のテーマを提示している。「レストランにて」の場合、詩劇風の第一、第二スタンザとより叙述的な第三スタンザは、明らかにフォームが異質であり、つながり方はぎくしゃくとしている。しかし、内容としては、文化人類学的、神話的世界を併置することによって、前の二つのスタンザを浮かび上がらせ、風刺し、対照することに成功している。スタンザとスタンザをつなぐ繋辞の役割をする表面的な言葉なしで、ある意味で「暴力的」ともいえる結合の仕方で結びつけられ、類推がしいられてはいるが、一つの詩としてしなやかな一体感を作り出している。これは後の『荒地』にも共通していて、「普通の意識以上のものを呼び起こす」エリオットの典型的な詩法の一つになっていくのである。『荒地』の草稿の中で、より論理的で散文的なスタイルの詩の数行が何箇所にもわたって、パウンドによって大胆にも削除されたことは、ファクシミリーの発見とその出版以来、周知のことになっているが、異質なものを併置することによって生み出される緊張感と類推によるテーマの統一感が重要視されているのである。類推という作業は読者に詩への参加を要求し、また、神話的手法と呼ばれる新しい詩作の方法は読者に博学の知識を求めることになった。このため詩の理解をより困難にしてしまったが、このような非常にアクティブな詩作方法はサンボリスムの芸術を継承したものであり、当時、T. E. ヒュームのイマジズムや古典主義の文学運動に傾倒していたパウンドの目指すところであった。

　1916年から1917年にかけて書かれたフランス語によるこれらの一連の詩は感動の詩というよりは美学的な関心の強さが感じられ、エリオットの習作時代におけるアーチザン（職人）としての才能を見ることができるよう

第一章　T.S.エリオット

に思われる。それはサンボリスムの詩との出会いから始まっているが、エリオットにとって、「詩は言葉そのものによって書かれるものだ」と言ったマラルメの純粋詩の詩法は究極的に賛同できるものではなかった。混沌の中に秩序を求める姿勢こそエリオットのモダニストとしての大きな特徴があったからである。それはイメジャリーを詩の核とし、想像力を重視したロマン主義の傾向を継承するものでありながら、個人の経験や感覚経験に依存するのではなくて、伝統やキリスト教の世界観を希求するものであった。しかしながら、語と語、行と行、スタンザとスタンザの相互浸透から生まれてくる静かなセンセーションやその効果の一過性というサンボリスムの特徴はエリオットの詩人としての生涯の最後まで消えることはなかった。そして、その詩法の根底には詩語をとりまくフォームの周到な選択があった。『荒地』は言うまでもなく、その後の『虚ろな人々』や『灰の水曜日』といった改宗前後の作品についてさえもエリオットは完全に満足げな発言はひかえている。揶揄している場合さえある。エリオット一流のポーズであるにしろ、言語と形式の感動に対する関係それ自体が新しいそのような詩の世界を提示しているのだ。それを彼自身の個性と限界としてみずから認めざるをえなくなったとき、エリオットは感動と美の芸術としての詩から、より客観的な伝達の機能を有する劇へと創作活動を転換させていくのである。フォームの観点から見てきた上記のフランス語で書かれた四つの詩は『荒地』に代表されるようなエリオットの偉大な没個性とも言うべき個性を形成するその過渡期にある重要な習作と言える。

注
1）ドミニック・ランセ著, 阿部良雄, 佐藤東洋麿共訳, 『十九世紀フランス詩』（文庫クセジュ, 白水社, 1991), 91.
2）cf.加藤美雄著, 『フランス象徴詩研究』（駿河台出版社, 1979), 第6章　トリスタン・コルビエールの詩集『黄色い恋』。
3）Eliot, T. S. *Collected Poems 1909-1962* (Faber & Faber, 1970), 13. 本論の引用はすべてこの版による。
4）Davie, Donald. *The End of an Era* (Macmillan, 1956); Casebook, 155.

詩形のエチュード

5) Eliot, T. S. *Sellected Essays* (Faber & Faber, 1972), 145.
6) エリオットの四つのフランス語による詩の日本語訳は深瀬基寛，上田保，鍵谷幸信氏のものを参考にさせていただいた。
7) cf.『フランス文学講座 3　詩』（大修館書店），259.
8) 窪田般若著，『ミラボー橋の下をセーヌが流れ——フランス詩への招待』，96-98。
9) 「コルビエールの墓碑銘」は次のようなものだが，エリオットの「あらゆるものの不義なる混合」よりも人生にたいする哀感と苦々しい思いが伝わってくる。

ÉPITAPHE *POUR* *TRISTAN JOACHIM-ÉDOUARD* 　*CORBIÈRE,* *PHILOSOPHE, ÉPAVE,* 　*MORT-NÉ*	*EPITAPH* *FOR* *TRISTAN JOACHIM-EDWARD* 　*CORBIERE,* *PHILOSOPHER, STRAY,* 　*STILL-BORN*
Mélange adultère de tout: De la fortune et pas le sou, De l'énergie et pas de force, La liberté, mais une entorse. Du coeur, du coeur! de l'âme, non − Des amis, pas un compagnon, De l'idée et pas une idée, De l'amour et pas une aimée, La paresse et pas le repos. Vertus chez lui furent défauts, Ame blasée inassouvie. Mort, mais pas guéri de la vie, Gâcheur de vie hors de propos Le corps à sec et la tête ivre, Espérant, niant l'avenir, Il mourut en s'attendant vivre Et vécut s'attendant mourir.	Everything's adulterous medley: Of fortune and without a penny, Of energy and without efficacy, Though bent, Liberty. Of heart, of heart! of soul, none − Of friends, but no true one, Of ideas but no idea, Of love and no beloved dear, Lazy without resting. Virtue in him defaulting, Blase soul hankering. Dead, but not cured of living, Bungler of life without scope The head soaked and the body dry, In denial of the future, hoped, With an expectation of life he died And lived expecting to die.

　　　　　　　　　　　　　　　　　from *THE CENTENARY*
　　　　　　　　　　　　　　　　　　　　CORBIERE

10）コルビエールは因習に反抗し，伝統的な詩型で詩を書くことを拒んだ詩人である。人生や文学をパロディ化する精神は，ラフオルグと共にエリオットに大きな影響を与えたと考えられる。しかし，エリオットはこの型破りの詩人の作品を模倣しながら古典のフォームを切り捨てることなく，簡潔で断片的な詩の創作に向かっている。
11）Preminger, Alex. ed., *Princeton Encyclopedia of Poetry and Poetics* (Princeton University Press, 1974), 11.
12）Eliot, T. S. *To Criticize the Critic* (New York: Farrar, Straus & Giroux, 1970), 184.
13）Eliot, *Selected Essays,* 424.
14）cf.ランセ,『十九世紀フランス詩』, 109.
15）Baudelaire, Charles. Les Fleurs du Mal (Paris: Garnier Frères, 1961), 13.
16）日本語訳は福永武彦，阿部良雄氏のものを参考にさせていただいた。

T.S. Eliot's *Journey of the Magi*
──Journey of the Soul to the Still Point──

> T. S. Eliot's poetry travels perhaps further and through more kinds of consciousness than that of any comparable poet.[1]
> Stephen Medcalf

> Eliot's symbolic configuration conflates three realms of reference - the fictional frame, the correspondences of Christian typology, and his own deepest and most troublesome feelings.[2]
> Ronald Bush

Losing the way in the middle of his life, Eliot's wandering causes, more or less, changes in his style of poetry as well as delicate alterations in his evaluation of writers in his criticism. After the despair in *The Hollow Men* (1925), Eliot's poetic style changes little by little with subjects rather religious than agnostic as in *The Waste Land*. According to John H. Timmerman, Eliot remarked that his poetry was over after *The Hollow Men*. Around this time his publisher started the series of 'Ariel' poems for Christmas to which he was to contribute.[3] His new start, however, could not make him easily find a new voice; a completely new theme and new way of expressing it. But considering the two years from the publication of *The Hollow Men* in 1925 to his baptism in 1927, the time of his personal upheavals and the crucial period in his life, we should give much attention to the works of his turning point. It is not only because they show new expressions of religious consciousness, but also because they have the structure of 'three realms' put together in order to recreate historical moments. Stephen Medcalf suggests Eliot's widening of consciousness in his poetry, and Ronald Bush, further, reveals the delicate, compound structure of the poet's mind. Eliot's journey of poetry shows us his still unsettled mind and unique aestheticism in *Ariel Poems*.

1. Construction of historical moment

One of the most distinguished differences between *Ariel Poems* and the earlier poems is that Eliot uses his historical sense not to make a poem of fragmentary patchwork, but to recover history in an artistic form. As Ronald Bush says, leaving the earlier style without context of history, and the mere juxtaposition of images or scenes, Eliot moves under Lancelot Andrewes. *Journey of the Magi* starts under the great influence of Andrewes:

> 'A cold coming we had of it,
> Just the worst time of the year
> For a journey, and such a long journey:
> The ways deep and the weather sharp,
> The very dead of winter.'[4]   (1-5)

Eliot cites the similar part of Andrewes' sermon in his essay.

> 'It was no summer progress. A cold coming they
> had of it at this time of the year, just the worst time
> of the year to take a journey, and specially a long

> journey in. The ways deep, the weather sharp, the
> days short, the sun farthes off, In solstitio brumali,
> "The very dead of winter."[5]

Eliot published his essay on Lancelot Andrewes in 1926 and praised his "intellect and sensibility in harmony" in his sermons higher than that of Donne. The alteration of evaluation corresponds to Eliot's transition in his poetical style. About Eliot's concern at this time, Gertrude Patterson concludes that Eliot's later poetry "deals with the actuality of believing; it is the poet's aim to find through the medium of his verse a way of expressing what it feels like to believe".[6] And Timmerman points out the origin and sources of the poems:

> Eliot develops more ordered patterns of symbolism. These
> originate in biblical sources in part, but also in the liturgal
> language of creeds, sacraments, and prayers.[7]

Here, we might recall the term "mythical method" which Eliot used in his criticism on Joyce's *Ulysses*. In the literature of Modernism, the mythical method has an important role and meaning:

> using myth, in manipulating a continuous parallel between
> contemporaneity and an antiquity... is simply a way of
> controlling, of ordering, of giving a shape and a significance
> to the immense panorama of futility and anarchy which is
> contemporary history.[8]

Eliot's new "mythical method" is different from the old one in *The Waste Land*. Eliot attemps to grasp the ineffability of belief by using biblical sources. The apparent modification of one of the Andrewes' sermons into dramatic verse at the beginning suggests another example of erudition, but the quotation is melted into the stream of the story by the narrator and hints no shadow of sermon at all.

> There were times we regretted
> The summer places on slopes, the terraces,
> And silken girls bringing sherbet.
> Then the camel men cursing and grumbling
> And running away, and wanting their liquor and women,
> . . .
> At the end we preferred to travel all night,
> Sleeping in snatches,
> With the voices singing in our ears, saying
> That this was all folly.   (8-12, 17-20)

His narrative technique is so real; using the phrase of Andrewes' sermon, it 'forces a concrete presence upon us.'[9] But the source of the precise images depicting the wealthy old life is *Anabase* by St. John Perse which Eliot translated from the French between 1926 and 1930. Eliot's use of others' works seems to help him make a new poetical world, although he has already said that a great writer steals, not borrows. Without quotation marks or letting know their sources, Eliot could develop the 'incantatory power of the passage' and transform the worlds of Andrewes and Perse. The 'idiosyncratic flavor' of the syntax and figures appears to correspond to the uneasiness of the post and the effect culminates in the anxiety of the last line: this journey might be 'all folly.' The first stanza of *Journey of the Magi* seems to be nothing but an old story of the troublesome journey. But Eliot creates his poetic world of the imagination with the precise and concrete, but alien images of the holy journey, and also masculine rhymes and staccato, so that he could suggest a journey 'at once geographical and spiritual,' and indicate 'the significance of a journey toward the interior.' The construction of historical moment begins without the familiar story of the Incarnation, but with the innocent, unexpectedly, doubtful mind about it.

2. Limit of the biblical symbolism

About the expression of nature or natural images in the Eliot's earlier poems, Susan M. Felch says,

> ... nature is an extension of the human situation ... man's decline has affected the entire natural world; cosmically, constellations are veiled and the seas themselves have shrunk.[10]

Eliot rejects a romantic view of nature, and he develops, she argues, 'an emblematic approach to elaborate the larger moral focus.' In the second stanza we have a natural description of the journey but with some hidden symbols.

> Then at dawn we came down to a temperate valley,
> Wet, below the snow line, smelling of vegetation,
> With a running stream and a water-mill beating the darkness,
> And three trees on the low sky.
> And an old white horse galloped away in the meadow. (21-25)

The readers are led to the biblical scene of the Passion through the imagery of three trees which suggest the death of Jesus at Calvary. But the crucial, historical moment is, we could say, under the reserved control of the poet. As Timmerman points out, the beginning of the second stanza establishes 'the personal regenaration' symbolized by the running stream and the dawning of a spiritual illumination as the water mill beats away the darkness. According to the Dantean colour symbology, the color white is assigned to the Old Testament; so we could decipher the last line like this: the fulfillment of the Old Testament law and prophecy as the past dispensation galloped away at the announcement of the Christ's birth. Here the unified moment hints of death and birth. The slight allusion to rebirth is through the biblical symbolism, but the symbolically described landscape is not the 'objective correlative' of powerful feeling. Yet the Magi go on their journey. Eliot's Magi appear to have no belief to support their activity.

The lines of the latter half of the second stanza are problematic, adding to the ambiguity of the preceding lines.

> Then we came to a tavern with vine-leaves over the lintel,
> Six hands at an open door dicing for pieces of silver,
> And feet kicking the empty wine-skin.
> But there was no information, and so we continued
> And arrived at evening, not a moment too soon
> Finding the place; it was (you may say) satisfactory.　　(26-31)

The narrator's monologue is still full of biblical allusions and symbols. Timmerman fully explains each symbol; for example, Jesus' naming himself as the True vine, Judas' barter with the Chief Priests for the silver to betray the Christ, and Jesus' reference to new wine put into old wineskins which is a parable of the passing of the old dispensation and the coming of the new in the Christ.[11] After the full explanation Timmerman says that they are a little too far-fetched, but the understatement and allusions are justified in the magus' meditation of the last stanza. The feeble symbolism covers the truth of the crucial historical moment. The words in parenthesis leave the impression of uneasiness about the realization of their arrival at 'the place' which is faithfully completed in the poem, 'not a moment too soon.' As to the dubious mind presented in the second stanza, Ronald Bush says:

> Writing to Virginia Woolf from Los Angels once, he (Eliot) told her that in America, to use the words of Anabase, "Doubt is cast on the reality of things." The same holds for everything Eliot introduces in the second stanza of "Journey of the Magi" ... the world of preconscious experience and the world of Christian exegesis. "Doubt is cast" by the poem on the significance of both.[12]

The artistic reconstruction of the *Journey of the Magi* is reconsidered using the feeble symbolism of the biblical world. The solidity of the natural setting is lost; it is neither distorted as in the earlier poems nor blessed in 'our first world' as in the later poetry. The Magi see and overlook the signs, and say 'I should be glad of another death.'

It is well known that Eliot started his poetic carrier under the influence of the French symbolism and the metaphyscal poets a little later. But in the distinction he draws in "Lancelot Andrewes" in 1926, he moves from Donne, who finds "an object which shall be adequate to his feelings," to Andrewes, who is "wholly absorbed in the object and therefore responds with the adequate emotion." He values, then, the self-conscious poetic symbols more than the natural object as the proper and perfect symbol. Ronald Bush calls attention to the remark by Eliot in 1931 and refers to his words about the ultimate direction of poetry: it is the destiny of all the words in a poem to approach the status of symbols. And he cites the Eliot's writing to make clear what the word tends to.

> Symbolism is that to which the word tends both in religion and in poetry; the incarnation of meaning in fact; and in poetry it is the tendency of the word to mean as much as possible. To find the word and give it the utmost meaning, in its place; to mean as many things as possible, to make it both exact and comprehensive, and really to unite the disparate and remote, to give them a fusion and pattern with the word, surely this is the mastery at which the poet aims … (and) no extravagance of a genuine poet can go so far over the border line of ordinary intellect as the Creeds of the Church.[13]

Symblism aims at the incarnation of meaning, in fact, in the religious tradition. What a symbol is seems, in the Eliot's view, to be closely connected with the capacity of the word in every respect, and a poet is assumed not to be allowed to go too far beyond the ordinary intellect into the world of personal symbols. He found once in the works of such French symbolist poets as Jules Laforgue, Tristan Cobiére, Charles Baudelaire or Stéphene Mallarmé, the inner personal, satisfactory, world. Most of those poets rejected the outer world by means of their personal symbols. Eliot's criticism of Donne's sermons as "means of self-expression" shows the same attitude as his disapproval of the Symbolists' personal worlds.

The problem of symbolism now moves to the limit of the biblical symbolism. The Magi don't recognize the signs, in the specific correspondence of their symbolic significance, in the landscape. The signs are symbols here, but the landscape is a mere landscape for them. The feebleness of the biblical symbolism, the meaning of which the Magi could not penetrate, might picture the difficulties that existed before them. It also reflects the hesitation or weakness of the poet's power of believing. The journey of the Magi to the Incarnation 'was (you may say) satisfactory.'

Timmerman, on the other hand, develops his understanding of the word "satisfactory". He argues that Eliot maybe employs it out of his study of philosophy, drawing upon the definition of a necessary and sufficient fulfillment of the signs given. He concludes that "satisfactory" might be a statement of resolute conviction. We find a profound understatement in Timmerman's next viewpoint. He assents that this conclusion parallels the pattern that Saint John of the Cross provides when the soul experiences the union with the divine. He cites Saint John's description of the qualities of the soul.

> As it journeys it is supported by no particular interior light of understanding, nor by any exterior guide, that it may receive satisfaction therefrom on this lofty road - yet its love alone, which beams at this time, and makes its heart long for the Beloved, is that which now moves and guides it... without its knowledge how or in what manner. (2. 25. 456)[14]

The very arduous journey itself is just the means through which the soul obtains satisfaction. The Magi, in the same way, receive satisfaction, however uncertain of the source of it they might be or however hard the process might be. Their longing for 'the Beloved' in the hard times is a reward and what might be called satisfaction; it could be predestined. Timmerman affirms the positive aspect of "satisfactory".

We find the difference between Ronald Bush and Timmerman as to the understanding of the biblical symbolism and Eliot's way of completing the historical moment. It is related to the change of function of symbols as the age moves on. A symbol has already lost its function as a sign, which has a meaning in a specific correspondence. The Biblical symbols 'have for centuries been culturally received as history,' Timmerman cites Daniel Harris' words, and they might 'in the continually changing present invoke the beginnings of Christianity'.[15] Ronald Bush, on the other hand, insists on the ambiguity of the Magus' belief and that the context might hint Eliot's lack of epiphanic experience.[16] He observes on Eliot's way of symbolic structure like this:

> Eliot's symbolic configuration conflates three realms of reference − the fictional frame, the correspondences of Christian typology, and his own troublesome feelings. And far from asserting the dominance of any of them, the poem opens up a field in which the question of reference is deliberately deferred.[17]

Eliot knows his strategy of this poem so well that, Bush argues, Eliot would allow this poem to become more of a game.[18] *Journey of the Magi* is completed as an event of historical moment leaving the question of reference. This is Eliot's personal way of recreating the historical moment and shows the limit of the biblical symbolism in his mind.

3. The still point of the Incarnation

As we have seen so far, the Magi continue this journey without knowing the meaning of the signs in the landscape and the narrator develops his style from monologue to meditation in the last two lines in the second stanza. The last stanza begins with a retrospective and more dramatic monologue.

> All this was a long time ago, I remember,
> And I would do it again, but set down
> This set down
> This: were we led all that way for
> Birth or Death? There was a Birth, certainly,
> We had evidence and no doubt. I had seen birth and death,
> But had thought they were different; this Birth was
> Hard and bitter agony for us, like Death, our death.　　(32-39)

The journey "ended satisfactory" and the narrator says he would do it again, but he enigmatically asks: "were we led all the way for/ Birth or Death?" He saw "Birth" and at the same time he saw "Death". This is a paradox and a kind of riddle. "Hard and bitter agony" is immediately associated with the Crucifixion, but the paradox which bewilders Magus, Timmerman stresses, inheres in Andrewes and he cites the Nativity Sermon of 1618 :

We may well begin with Christ in the cratch; we must end with Christ on the Cross. The cratch is the sign of the cross. They that write *de re rustica,* describe the form of making a cratch cross-wise. The scandal of the cratch is a good preparative to the scandal of the Cross...−. 'primo ne discrepet imum'; 'that His beginning and His end may suit well and not disagree'...[19]

The Magus refers neither to the crèche nor to the cross, just as he did not notice the sign of 'the three trees on the low sky.' But the same paradox makes him ill 'at ease in the old dispensation' and long for 'another death.' Timmerman tells us that it is this paradox that Andrewes celebrates as the miracle of the nativity. There are only a few steps left to reach the poetical world of *Four Quartets*: 'In my beginning is my end. In my end is my beginning.' The problem is that Eliot at this time hesitates to create the still point of the Incarnation artistically; more correctly, to fix a story of a miracle in a poetical form. His concern is to represent what believing is, but he does not use his personal symbols. Unlike Hopkins he could not find a new voice, and he had to explain to himself discursively the truth of his mind. The creation of the still point in a poetical form here depends on the Incarnation alone. Having received his own baptism only weeks before writing this poem, his spiritual journey moves from agnosticism to skepticism and at last to affirmation of Christian belief. But his poetical development causes this poem to end 'not with a bang but a whimper.' We know Eliot's actuality of believing through the analysis on Eliot's symbolic configuration and his trial of construction of the historical moment.

NOTES
1) Medcalf, Stephen. "Eliot and the Punk Aesthetic," TLS (June 7, 1996), 13.
2) Bush, Ronald. *T. S. Eliot: A Study in Character and Style* (Oxford UP, 1983), 128.
3) Timmerman, Johan H. *T. S. Eliot's Aeriel Poems: The Poetics of Recovery*

(Lewisburg: Bucknell UP , 1994), 17.
4) Eliot, T.S. *Collected Poems 1909-1962*, (Faber & Faber 1970), 109. All the subsequent citations of Eliot's poems are to this edition.
5) Eliot, T.S. *Selected Essays*, (Faber & Faber 1972) , 350.
6) Patterson, Gertrude. *T. S. Eliot: Poems in the Making*, (Manchester UP, 1971), 182.
7) Timmerman, 25.
8) Kermode, Frank. ed., *Selected Prose of T. S. Eliot*, (Faber & Faber1975), 177.
9) Eliot, *Selected Essays*, 350.
10) Fetch, Susan M. "Nature as Emblem: Natural Images in T.S. Eliot's Earlier Poetry." *YEATS ELIOT REVIEW* (Fall, 1992), 90.
11) Timmerman, 76-77.
12) Bush, 128.
13) Bush, 124.
14) Timmerman, 78.
15) Timmerman, 82.
16) Bush, 129.
17) Bush, 128.
18) Bush, 129.
19) Timmerman, 85.

Recognition and Ambivalence in *Marina*

T. S. Eliot's notion of poetic figuration altered in the nineteen-twenties quite a lot. As with so many of his stylistic transformations, his enthusiasm for literary aestheticism developed through an encounter with other poets. It is Shakespeare's parable of rebirth and transcendent plane that Eliot is drawn to at the time of his conversion, as well as Dante. Eliot admires Shakespeare's own spiritual metamorphosis in his plays. His interest in Shakespeare's plays lasts from his late twenties to late thirties. *Marina* is one of Eliot's short poems, written and published in 1930. Eliot bases it on one of the dramatic moments in *Pericles*. The problem in reading *Marina*, which is generally highly estimated as a joyous poem, is the ambiguity of the context as a whole and the way of development of the recognition scene. Is it possible to say that the poem is successful in expressing a kind of ecstasy and the state of unconsciousness entering the world beyond? It is a poem at his controversial period, and some critics reveal the lack of Eliot's epiphanic experience. It is important to recognize the ambivalence of joy and agony in this poem in which we can see Eliot's struggle for the recovery from his *Purgatory*.

Marina and 'Recognition'

Many critics have proclaimed *Marina* as Eliot's most "joyous" poem, but as J. H. Timmerman suggests in his book: *T. S. Eliot's Aeriel Poems: The Poetics of Recovery* (1994), we have to be attentive to the shadows of anguish in his works even after the conversion. It should be made clear and explained in detail that the joy or vision of new life is not separated from agony. The significance of his poetry after 1927 exists in the change of his suffering. He struggles with his stern moral consciousness in order to gain the reality of the world beyond. Few critics, including Timmerman, have ever made full description of this attractive short poem, and I'd like to make clear that the significance of this poem lies in Eliot's ambivalence in describing his bliss.

T. S. Eliot says in The New York Times (1953) that he thought his poetry was over after *The Hollow Men*... but writing the Ariel poems released a stream which led directly to *Ash Wednesday*. His recovery from despair started through Geoffrey Faber's invitation in 1927 to contribute to 'Ariel Poems', a series of illustrated Christmas greetings pamphlets priced at one shilling. The results are *Journey of the Magi* in 1927, *A Song for Simeon* in 1928, *Animula* in 1929 and *Marina* in 1930. The following two poems, published in 1931 and 1932, are put together in *Coriolan* and included in 'Unfinished Poems', not in 'Ariel Poems', in the complete edition by his choice. It reflects Eliot's restlessness to create a new form during his spiritual pilgrimage.

Marina is generally considered to be the ultimate "joyous" poem in 'Ariel Poems'. Eliot comments on it in a lecture given in 1937: 'to my mind the finest of all the "recognition scenes" is Act v, i of that very great play *Pericles*. It is a perfect example of the "ultra-dramatic", a dramatic action of beings who are more than human ... or rather, seen in a light more than that of day.[1] The recognition scene of *Pericles* stimulated Eliot to write *Marina*. The reunion of Pericles and Marina is on one stage of "the mystery of life" and the miracle is completed with

第一章　T. S. エリオット

the oracle by the goddess, Diana, in his dream just after the shock of sudden revelation of his lost daughter. The highest emotional scene of this romance is the reunion of the father and daughter. Shakespeare wrote many recognition scenes in his life, and especially those in his later romantic plays should be understood as the stages of reconciliation of a man with this world or with his own life. Charles Warren cites Wilson Knight's *Myth and Miracle* and says Knight "presses very hard for recognition of *Pericles* as a great work".[2] Knight also points out recognition in Shakespeare's late plays is generally "offering the consummate philosophical resolution to problems explored in the tragedies." A recognition scene or the meaning of recognition is very important when we take Shakespeare's works as a whole and consider them as a development of his career, as Eliot admits such a modern interpretation in the introduction of *The Wheel of Fire*. We know the struggles of Shakespeare's tragic heroes and their stages of recognition before catharsis. Frank Kermode says Shakespeare's recognition scenes seem to have become "almost the principal reason for writing plays."[3] And in Eliot's *Marina* we know his whole enterprise was to see what kind of poem could be made out of the recognition scene alone, because Eliot's scheme here is poetic construction of a moment of revelation only through Pericles' recognition.

　Recognition is a regular feature of dramatic plots and Kermode points out the importance of the recognition scene especially in *Pericles* and says that it is certainly one of Shakespeare's "carefully composed" scenes. He describes the usage and the definition of "recognition" from the classics. We can get the idea of what recognition is in a drama.

> 　Aristotle treated recognition (*anagnorisis*) as that part of the plot which presented "a change from ignorance to knowledge,"

> a change produced by what he called *peripeteia,* a reversal or turning point: the moment when the direction of the story is altered in preparation for the recognition that, "against expectation," as Aristotle puts it, brings it to an end by discovering at last its true course, hitherto concealed.[4]

Eliot is in his fourth poem of 'Ariel Poems' : *Marina* involved in the visionary aspect of the recognition scene rather than the mere romantic development of the play. Pericles' change from ignorance to knowledge was a good resource of his poem when Eliot had almost resigned writing a poem. Eliot shows the conversion story of himself, Lyndall Gordon says, "irresolute in *The Hollow Men* (1923-5); ill-at-ease in the 'old dispensation' after his conversion in *Journey of the Magi* (August 1927); waiting in *Ash Wednesday* (December 1927-April 1930)." It follows that, as some critics point out, Eliot had to undergo a religious experience before he could write some new verse and validate his new life. Gordon cites Eliot's confession from the pulpit of King's Chapel in Boston in 1932:

> words had to wait on religious experience which one could not will. A godly and devout life would not suffice, only the strongest and deepest feelings helped by moments of insight, clarification, and crystallization which come but seldom.

He has to wait for a moment of religious experience which we cannot intend to have. His scheme is to make use of the recognition scene in this romance to create a vision and to shape a work of art out of it. He was at that time on the way to finding a new method to communicate his work, not in poetry, but in a style of more raw material, a drama. Eliot's *Marina* is a soliloquy by Pericles. In 1930 Eliot wrote an introduction for Wilson Knight's *The Wheel of Fire*, remarking that Shakespeare has "'something to say," a "deeper pattern" below the level of plot and character. This is the "poet's world," a "vision," he says.

Recognition leads, in Eliot's words, to a vision. *Marina* is a typical example with which he tried to present a vision in an artistic form. Eliot has "something to say" through the dramatization of the moment of recognition.

In *Marina* we can see the poet's vision connected closely with the extreme joy of Pericles, which stands for bliss in his theology, just like the blissful scene of laughing children in the rose garden in *Burnt Norton*. It is the recovery of innocence which is an extreme joy represented in his vision. The scene of recovery of innocence are so calm and peaceful. They are far from the dry, dark, obscure images which are characteristic of many earlier poems of Eliot's. A child is, from a psychological point of view, the synthesis of conscious and unconscious elements in one's personality. It is therefore "a symbol that unites the opposites; a mediator, bringer of healing." A child symbolizes perfect happiness and belongs to another world in Eliot's late poems. We are led to Pericles' dramatic monologue which should be full of joy and bliss.

To *Marina* is, however, added an extremely tragic epigraph cited from *Hercules Furens* by Seneca. Unlike other four "Ariel" poems, *Marina* has an epigraph. What is Eliot's intention of this epigraph? What is its effect on the poem as a whole? We are at the door looking into Eliot's agony, as Timmerman suggests, even in his poetry just after the conversion. Timmerman agrees with Elizabeth Drew's comment on Eliot's "mythical method" as an attempt to grasp "the ineffability of belief" through a poetic story or drama and declares:

> the Magus in the previous "Ariel Poem" has no theological framework by which to understand and assimilate such events. In a sense, he is still a bit like Gerontion, pondering the sign that is given but ill equipped to interpret the sign.
> ... the Magus has, nonetheless, given himself over emotionally to an acceptance of a paradox he doesn't fully understand.[5]

It is crucial to ascertain the significance and delicateness of the undercurrent of each Eliot's poem after the conversion. Like the Magus who wants another death because he has certainly seen the birth (death) of the saviour though he cannot understand it, Eliot has to be satisfied with his conversion if "it was (you may say) satisfactory." While examining Pericles' recognition scene created by Eliot, we are to realize the ambivalence of Eliot's mind even after the conversion. We will see Pericles' recognition of bliss and another unknown terror, the co-existence of them in the lines.

Epigraph in *Marina*

Marina begins with the utterance of Pericles' joy and doubt at the time when he finally finds and recognises Marina before his eyes as his long lost daughter. It is a miracle for him who has experienced many adventures and suffered great losses. In Shakespeare's *Pericles*, he complains to the gods who have taken away all his joys and happiness, and given him hard trials one after another.

> O you gods!
> Why do you makes us love goodly gifts,

And snatch them straight away?
(3.1. 22-24)

His internal tempest rages and he swears at the "disconsolation" which could not be cured at all by anybody. The recognition scene in *Marina* is slowly unfolded through his monologue. The discovery of his daughter softens his mind and loosens the memory of his past. What he remembers first of all is the landscape of the sea and the images of the seashore.

What seas what shores what grey rocks and what islands
What water lapping the bow
And scent of pine and the wood thrush singing through the fog
What images return
O my daughter.[6]　　(1-5)

Eliot writes these lines with two plays in his mind, *Pericles* by Shakespeare and *Hercules Furens* by Seneca. The epigraph often seen in Eliot's poems is one of the main characteristics of his poetry as well as the enormous volume of notes of *The Waste Land*. Eliot uses an epigraph as an important part of a poem. His fundamental method as a modernist poet is a Symbolist method. His extreme way of presenting items is to put fragments side by side. He intends to indicate a special state of mind caused by putting fragments together. F. H. Bradley claimes that the self is a construct that is generally derived from experience and Eliot agrees with him on this point. By using an epigraph, we can conclude, Eliot tries to create a unique self and reveals the ambivalence of his own mind.

　The works by Seneca, a Roman writer, are considered to have

been a great stimulus to Elizabethan drama and they were popular among the people through their translation. Seneca's tragedies became the foundation of the Elizabethan drama especially with the allegorical aspect developed. Eliot cites two lines from Seneca's tragedy, *Hercules Furens* (1138) as his epigraph.

> *Quis hic, quae*
> *Regio, quae mundi plaga?*[7]

We know the contrast between two plays. The echo of Seneca's tragedy gives an ominous shadow to the main lines of *Marina*, but the poem unexpectedly reveals the pleasant bewilderment of Pericles. We can find one of Eliot's intentions in this poem, as he tells us about it in a letter dated 9 May 1930.

> I intend a criss-cross between Pericles finding alive, and Hercules finding dead – the two extremes of the recognition scene.

Pericles' way of overcoming inner death by resigning this world should be contrasted to the deadly life of Hercules as a murderer. The difference between two recognition scenes is obvious. Pericles is concerned with the revelation as a miraculously wonderful experience. But in *Hercules Furens* the hero, Hercules, has been driven mad as a punishment for his pride and emerges from insanity to discover horror. The epigraph reminds us of Hercules, a hero, awakening from the spell of madness under which he kills his wife and children. When he awakens, he is astonished at the dreadful sight and at the fact that it is actually what he has done. What Seneca's tragedy conveys to us is 'pride' as the greatest sin of man and the horror as a punishment given by the furious god. Hercules is not allowed redemption; he is deprived of it. Seneca's philosophy is for Eliot incomplete. Eliot points out Seneca's influence upon Shakespeare's plays and criticizes the lack of virtue in his characters. He says, for example, about Othello's last speech, which is one version of 'cheering oneself up.'

> He (Othello) is endeavouring to escape reality, he has ceased to think about Desdemona, and is thinking about himself. Humility is the most difficult of all virtues to achieve; nothing dies harder than the desire to think well of oneself.[8]

Othello tries to avoid looking at reality and he is involved in keeping his reputation even after his death. It is a terrible 'exposure of human weakness,' Eliot says in *Shakespeare and the Stoicism of Seneca* in 1927, adding that "the Roman stoicism is an important ingredient in Elizabethan drama." The presence of the greatest virtue, humility, is a major concern for Eliot at the time of his conversion.

> The original stoicism, and especially the Roman stoicism, was of course a philosophy suited to slaves; hence its absorption into early Christianity ... Stoicism is the refuge for the individual in an indifferent or hostile world too big for him; it is the permanent substratum of a number of versions of cheering oneself up. Nietzsche is the most conspicuous modern instance of cheering oneself up. The stoical attitude is the reverse of Christian humility. [9]

The lack of humility, as Eliot stresses in his criticism on *Othello*, causes the punishment on Hercules by the god in this Roman tragedy. The most distinctive feature of Seneca's tragedy is the god's anger and the unavoidable punishment on man. The spell of madness is beyond Hercules' ability and he is helpless. His agony tells us about the absolute, mighty existence over human beings. A discovery of horror by the hero in the epigraph throws a cloud of despair, which has something in common with the 'disconsolation' of Pericles. The epigraph is a shadowy fragment and constitutes one part of the poem which is a deep undercurrent in *Marina*. When we think about his making of this poem and the addition of an epigraph, we can say that Eliot is unexpectedly revealing his anticipation even when uttering and expressing extreme joy. Besides the allegorical meaning in this poem, *Marina* as a whole suggests another aspect and interpretation. The carefully-intended and deliberate stanzas show some characteristics of his poetry and theology, and we are going to find out in this paper whether Pericles' pilgrimage could be completed or not, and whether *Marina* should be acceptable as a 'joyous poem' with no shade as a whole, or not.

Pilgrimage in *Marina*

Pericles' awakening from 'disconsolation' starts with the description of the sea whose images remind him of the past terrible memories. He is now at the sea again in his mind, hearing the lap at the ship bow and scenting the pines of the seashore. He takes another voyage to 'a higher reality,' clearing the disastrous past. The next fragment is full of symbolic usage about the people around him, borrowing images from *Purgatory* by Dante.

Those who sharpen the tooth of the dog, meaning
Death

> Those who glitter with the glory of the hummingbird, meaning Death
> Those who sit in the sty of contentment, meaning Death
> Those who suffer the ecstasy of the animals, meaning Death   (6-13)

The deliberate, decorative and repetitive lines emphasize the strength of Pericles' hatred toward the people who live in this secular world. He is accusing the people whom he had met and fought with in the past, but Eliot makes it universal by making use of Dantean images. Eliot called the people living in this futile world 'unreal people' in 'an unreal city' in *The Waste Land* in 1922. His negative sensibility now turns into the conviction that those people are 'death-meaning' people. In order to define such 'death-bringing' behaviours, Eliot borrows four of the Seven Roots of sinfulness from *Purgatory*. Eliot's contemporised figures of the four great sins do "not have any precise counterpart in the Purgatorio," but they clearly evoke certain "root stains."

> The Seven Roots — Pride, Envy, Wrath, Sloth, Avarice, Gluttony, and Lust are not the actual sins, but constitute the humanly ineradicable taint of sin that affects the will. The taints are manifested, then, in the behaviours of sin.[10]

Eliot chooses the figures whose root stains are gluttony, pride, sloth, and lust and seems to have avoided wordy repetition of all seven sins. He makes a big space in each line as if to hasten and impress the oblivion of his past. He is beginning to recognise the discovery of his daughter as grace rather than miracle. His recognition is different from Hercules' awakening from the spell to find himself a murderer. The next fragment begins with no subjects.

> Are become unsubstantial, reduced by wind,
> A breath of pine, and the woodsong fog
> By this grace dissolved in place   (14-16)
> . . .

The people condemned to death don't have their substances any more and they are invisibly melting into the sea-scenery for Pericles. Grace, Donald Coggan says in *The Heart of the Christian Faith* in 1978, often takes the form of forgiveness by God. Pericles cannot see the people "meaning death" any longer, for he is also a man going to receive forgiveness. In the visible and also invisible world, he experiences the restoration of innocence. The adherence to the sea-scenery tells us the significance of the symbols in the poetry of Eliot. All the water combines to absolve the torment of the human world.

> What is this face, less clear and clearer
> The pulse in the arm, less strong and stronger —
> Given or lent? More distant than stars and nearer than the eye
>
> Whispers and small laughter between leaves and hurrying feet
> Under sleep, where all the water meet.   (17-21)

"The emotional equivalent of thought" in poetry is one of the key words in Eliot's aestheticism of literature, and he says "to express precise emotion requires as great intellectual power as precise thought." He is now expressing "a vision, a dream if you like." Timmerman approves of *Marina* as a poem of a moment of joyous encounter with grace.

> In this remarkable recognition moment in *Marina*, Eliot achieves that precise expression of joy, the sheer emotional wonder of restoration that escapes rational analysis.[11]

The expression at the moment of recognition is similar to that of the first scene of the three witches in *Macbeth*. B. C. Southam points it out as one example of Eliot's assimilation of other works, which might be called Eliot's "progressive imitation."

> Eliot seems to be combining this allusion with verbal echoes of the scene in Shakespeare's *Macbeth* (I.iii): on the Heath the first Witch greets Banquo as 'Lesser than Macbeth, and the greater'; and the second Witch, 'Not so happy, yet much happier.' Banquo, like Eliot's Pericles, questions the nature of what he sees.[12]

The witches' speeches are riddles with contradictory words. This is rhetorically called an oxymoron. Eliot is imitating this usage in order to express Pericles' mental movement between the world of reason and the world without, transmuting the scene into an innocent, blissful landscape. It is a scene of vision and a moment of bliss, which develops into the expressions like "Whispers and small laughter between leaves and hurrying feet", "our first world" and "the rose garden" in *Burnt Norton*.

Pericles in his vision states clearly the conditions of his old ship. The lines describe the ruined ship and he declares his rebirth by resigning his life. The real, pictureresque description of the ship is alternated three times with his emotional longing for his rebirth. They constitute the longest fragment of this poem.

> <u>Bowsprit cracked with ice and paint cracked with heat.</u>
> I made this, I have forgotten
> And remember.
> <u>The rigging weak and the canvas rotten</u>
> <u>Between one June and another September.</u>
> Made this unknowing, half conscious, unknown, my own.
> <u>The garboard strake leaks, the seams need caulking.</u>
> This form, this face, this life
> Living to live in a world of time beyond me; let me
> Resign my life for this life, my speech for that unspoken,
> The awakened, lips parted, the hope, the new ships.   (22-32)
>   (underlines added)

His vision develops the old ship representing himself and the new life represented by Marina. In the original story by Shakespeare, Pericles mentions nothing of his being an old ship. But he now identifies himself with an old ship which is not a landscape any more. The repetition of "this" is distinctive to show the process of his recognition and emphasises the amazement, but Marina, his daughter, never appears in this poem. She is a kind of 'idea' like Beatrice for Dante. She is an existence to be sung lyrically and her role is "a kind of spiritual anima." Elizabeth Drew observes that "she is 'opalescent,' a semi-visionary companion, yet holding within her the *meaning* of the total experience."[13] The poet has to make his ideal lady both visible and invisible. But the more "this" is repeated, the more isolated, on the contrary, Pericles appears. Eliot allows himself discursiveness in his lines for the highest emotional scene. While the repetition of "this" might be telling the depth of his past despair and agony, it suggests the distance from the real world which he had renounced. But it is still ambiguous and questionable whether Pericles is uttering the monologue in a state of unconsciousness, having already left this world. Ronald Bush reveals the wall of self-consciousness dissolving during Pericles' declaration of resignation from this world.

> In "Marina," crystallised or figured by the recognition of his daughter, the experience of Eliot's speaker corresponds to a sudden assurance of the solidity of the world outside him. The poem enacts a miraculous dissolution of his diseased self-consciousness, ... Finally convinced of the world's reality, he is on the point of recognising his own.[14]

One meaning of recognition, Bush points out, is recognising reality with the wall of self-consciousness broken down. Pericles' recognition is recognition of bliss caused by the reappearance of his daughter, and, at the same time, of his own deep self-consciousness. Pericles' realisation of the outer world leaves him no place to go. The unknown world is coming near to him. Eliot's Pericles feels terror just after the moment of bliss.

> What seas what shores what granite islands towards my timbers
> And woodthrush calling through the fog
> My daughter.   (33-35)

Where Pericles intends to go he doesn't know. It is coming nearer towards him, not his ship going forward. The last three lines sound ambivalent, not enough to impress on us his conviction and decision. But they are truly showing Pericles' feelings and his mind of ambivalence. Bush says the pilgrimage of Pericles' soul is not completed.

> Like the three *Ariel* poems that precede it – "Journey of the Magi," "A song for Simeon," and "Animula" – "Marina" presents the feeling of a man in the process of dying to one life and unable to be born into another.[5]

The repetition of "this" reveals ironically the uneasiness of his mind. "This" is, after repeated several times, replaced with "that." It suggests the distance. Marina and her people will live there as "the new ships."

Eliot wrote about this poem to E. McKnight, who provided the poem with drawings: "I don't know whether it is any good at all. The theme is paternity; with a criss-cross between the text and the quotation."[16] The conciliation with the disastrous past appears to have been completed through the strong bondage between father and daughter, which is restored as a grace. Pericles hears a "calling" voice from some other world. The old ship is coming nearer to the shore of the unknown world. The last three lines are a little modified and shortened expression of the beginning of this poem. The reader knows the delicate difference of Pericles' mind after the recognition. The wonder at the beginning is changed into anxiety for the future. The pilgrimage of his soul from deep despair seems to have been done through the oblivion of his past and recovering innocence. The recognition is a great occasion to give the route of life "the true course." But Pericles still doesn't know what shore he is sailing to. Gower, a storyteller who guides us in Sakespeare's *Pericles*, assumes "man's infirmities" and for him the issue is "whether human life is subject to the mere whim of external

Events" or whether "some pattern directs events to preordained end."[17] Shakespeare leaves the choice to the audience's imagination, but Eliot has to create his Pericles as a person who could afford to receive bliss, because Eliot is impressed with this drama not only as a romantic play, but as an "ultra-dramatic" play of a man of conversion. Eliot's Pericles finds, though, another terror after coming back to reality, because he has no lady, nor 'idea,' to lead him. Marina is his daughter and she is also a "new ship." Eliot still does not possess his own religious conviction. We are susceptible of the shadow of the epigraph — another unknown terror Eliot creates in *Marina*.

Suspension of Joy in *Marina*

The last three lines in *Marina* present an ambiguous conclusion. They are the repetition of the beginning with a little difference. Pericles, who is regarding himself as an old ship, mentions mending his ship and hesitates to negate the uncertainty in his mind. This indicates his weakness to support the will and joy to meet the world beyond. He is now leaving his Purgatory and has expressed his vision. But the woodthrush *calling* is not quite pleasant for him to listen to. A. D. Moody writes that the contraction of the opening two lines into 'what seas what shores what granite islands towards my timbers', leads to a sense of menace.[18] He even suggests the woodthrush calling through the fog might be luring to shipwreck. We know the last short line "My daughter" is not incantation or joy. The undercurrent beneath the whole progress of Eliot's Pericles' recognition scene is deep and subtle. Eliot probably knew his scheme and intended the result. But the ambivalence of this poem shows us the reality of his struggle trying to liberate himself from the oppressive world of self-consciousness.

The problematic *Marina* might be the work which tests his epiphanic experience to support and validate his new life. His spiritual world and his belief developed in *Marina* seem to disclose one unliberated inner mind hidden under the theme of recognition.

REFERENCE BOOKS

Eliot, T. S. *Collected Poems* 1909-1962, (Faber & Faber, 1970).

Eliot, T. S. *Selected Essays,* (Faber & Faber, 1970).

Bush, Ronald. *T. S. Eliot: A Study in Character and Style* (Oxford UP, 1983).

Drew, Elizabeth. *T. S. Eliot: The Design of His Poetry* (Scribner's, New York, 1949).

Gordon, Lyndall. *Eliot's New Life* (Oxford UP, 1989).

Kermode, Frank. *Shakespeare's Language* (Penguin books, 2000).

Knight, G. Wilson. *The Wheel of Fire* (Oxford UP, 1930).

Larrissy, Edward. *Reading Twentieth-Century Poetry* (Basil Blackwell Ltd, Oxford, 1990).

Moody, A. D. *Thomas Sterns Eliot Poet* (Cambridge University Press, 1979).

Southam, B. C. *A Student Guide to the Selected Poems of T. S. Eliot* (Faber&Faber, 1994).

Timmerman, Johan H. *T. S. Eliot's Aeriel Poems: The Poetics of Recovery* (Lewisburg: Bucknell UP, 1994).

Warren, Charles. *T. S. Eliot on Shakespeare* (UMI Research Press, Michigan, 1987).

NOTES

1) Southam, B, C. *A Student Guide to the Selected Poems of T. S. Eliot* (Faber & Faber, 1994, 246).
2) Warren, Charles. *T. S. Eliot On Shakespeare* (UMI Research Press, Michigan 1987, 67).
3) Kermode, Frank. *Shakespeare's Language* (Penguin books, 2000, 260).

第一章　T. S. エリオット

4）Kermode, 256.
5）Timmerman, Johan H. *T. S. Eliot's Aeriel Poems: The Poetics of Recovery* (Lewisburg: Bucknell UP 1994), 91.
6）Eliot, T. S. *Collected Poems 1909-1962*, (Faber & Faber 1970), 115.
7）Eliot, *Collected Poems* 1909-1962, 115.
    cf. Southam's translation: 'What is this place, what country, what region of the world?' (246).
8）Eliot, T. S. *Selected Essays*, (Faber & Faber 1972), 130.
9）Eliot, *Selected Essays*, 131-132.
10）Timmerman, 146.
11）Timmerman, 149.
12）Southam, 248.
13）Drew, Elizabeth, *T. S. Eliot: The Design of His Poetry* (Scribner's, New York, 1949), 129.
14）Bush, Ronald. *T. S. Eliot: A Study in Character and Style* (Oxford Up.1983), 166.
15）Bush, 167.
16）Southam, 247.
17）Timmerman, 143.
18）Moody, A, D. *Thomas Sterns Eliot: Poet* (Cambridge University Press, 1979), 156.

第二章

ウィルフレッド・オウェン

Chapter 2 Wilfred Owen

Wilfred Owen's War Poetry:

──Pity, Beauty and Horror of the Transitional Poet──

John Silkin quotes from John H. Johnston's words and says in his book, *Out of Battle,* that "the poetry of modern warfare may be in the pity; but neither pity nor self-pity in themselves can inspire great poetry" (Silkin, *Battle* 197). Wilfred Owen's war poems, however, have attracted many readers' attention and have been loved for a long time. The poet and his works are, generally speaking, famous for the emphasis on pity toward soldiers and their fate on the battlefield. Pity was declared by the poet himself to precede the value of his own poetry in the preface of his anthology. He has gained the reputation of being the greatest poet of World War I, but his work has not been without any unfavorable remarks or revaluation by some critics and poets.

Owen's reputation has grown steadily since the first selection of his poems appeared under Siegfried Sassoon's editorship in 1920. He is, by common consent, the greatest English poet of World War I. But in 1924, as Bernard Bergonzi writes, the celebrated patriotic poet, Sir Henry Newbolt, said of Owen's poetry: "I don't think these shell-shocked war poems will move our grandchildren greatly – there's nothing fundamental or final about them" (Bergonzi, *Twilight* 117). He prefers perfect acceptance, which means perfect faith, to the ambiguity and skepticism of Owen. Newbolt continues: "Owen and the rest of the broken men rail at the Old Men who sent the young to die: they have suffered cruelly, but in the nerves and not the heart." We know that the implicit and unexamined premise the civilians accepted without question was underlying Newbolt's remarks. They believed in the military struggle unavoidable. The sense of alienation was most painfully felt when young soldies had to face the older people's incomprehension, ignorance, and belief in official propaganda. Newbolt chose paternal responsibility suffering from the ultimate agonies of young officers toward their men and of older men to their sons. He claims: "Paternity apart, what Englishman of fifty wouldn't far rather stop the shot himself than see the boys do it for him?" The cleavage in thinking between generations was vivid in the many poems written at that time and Owen's work was not the exception. He writes in *The Parable of the Old Man and the Young:*

> Then Abram bound the youth with belts and straps,
> And builded parapets and trenches there,
> And stretched forth the knife to slay his son.
> When lo! An angel called him out of heaven,
> Saying, Lay not thy hand upon the the lad,
> Neither do anything to him. Behold,
> A Ram, caught in a thicket by its horns;
> Offer the ram of Pride instead of him.
> But the old man would not so, but slew his son,
> And half the seed of Europe, one by one. (7-16)
>
> (Owen's poem is to Silkin's edition.)

His cry and protest against the war here borrow a story from the Bible which he once studied. He had already abandoned the religious life. He says in one letter to his mother that he had "murdered my false creed... the still false creeds that hold the hearts of nearly all my fellow men." Is his agony "in the nerves and not the heart" as Newbolt says? But Newbolt exactly points out a kind of reverse of heroism in Owen's poetry.

> I [Newbolt] like better Sassoon's two-sided collection — there are more than two sides to this question of war, and a man is hardly normal any longer if he comes to one. S. S. says that Owen pitied others but never himself: I'm afraid that isn't quite true — or at any rate not quite fair... (Bergonzi, *Twilight* 117)

It is true that Owen's range of poetry is narrow and his concern is exclusively and deliberately about suffering. At the beginning of his collection, he presented the famous declaration of his own poetry:

> Above all I am not concerned with Poetry.
> My subject is War, and the pity of War.
> The Poetry is in the pity. (Silkin xxxix)

The conscious restriction of the poetry range by Owen and the supportive words by Siegfried Sassoon might have been understood to be some means to claim a reputation as a great poet. But as William Empson said that all great poetry must in some way embody ambiguity, Owen's 'Herculean' world of ideas is not the expression of a simple idea. The favorable criticism for Owen also met with Yeats' crucial decision and Owen's poems were excluded from *the Oxford Book of Modern Verse* (1936) on the ground that passive suffering was not a proper subject for poetry. Yeats used Owen, Bergonzi says, as a stick to beat the Leftist poets of the 1930s who had adopted Owen as a progenitor of their direction. Bergonzi even hints the jealous attitude of Yeats toward the rich and roughly matured style of Owen's poetry.

The criticism against the high reputation of Owen's poetry leads us to two fundamental questions: one is whether pity and passive suffering can be a proper subject for poetry from the poetical view point, and the second is what the significance of Owen's poems is at all. When we hear that war poetry had established its own genre after World War I and it became popular among many readers, it is of great importance to reconsider Wilfred Owen's poetry from the standpoint of the these questions and also from the cultural situation of those days.

Wilfred Owen was born on March 18, 1893 with the religious background of the Church of England. He failed to get the scholarship to go to university and became the pupil and assistant of the Reverend Herbert Wigan at Dunsden Vicarage, Oxfordshire. Some early awakening of his conscience appears in this period through his contact with others' sufferings in the community. Silkin tells us that Owen's bitter experience obviously produced the two principal impulses in his poetry: pity and indignation. The references in his letters to the dissatisfaction with the surroundings reflect the recognition of his position and his inability to change the conditions of men's lives. This early social awareness makes us realize that Owen was not a poet for whom the war alone started such a compassionate awakening, and that without this awareness there would not have been such a great conscientious poet. What the war did for him was to awaken the sensitive young man's conscience, and to hasten the fusion of his lyrical sentiment with social awareness.

In September 1913, he started teaching at the Berlitz School of Languages in Bordeaux, and he met Laurent Tailhade in August 1914. Like Owen he had been intended for the church, but revolted against Christianity. He was a confirmed pacifist and the author of two pamphlets, *Lettre aux Conscrits* (1903) and *Pour la Paix* (1909), which caused a considerable disturbance. Owen was invited to his lecture at the Casino in Bagnères and the meeting was momentous for him. It was one of his three crucial encounters with living poets; the other two were with Harriet Monroe in 1915-16 and Siegfried Sassoon in 1917. Dominic Hibberd, who wrote an outstandingly good biography of Owen in 2002, reveals the fact that the French poet was a very important influence on him. Tailhade was a committed pacifist who influenced Owen to reject war, but Hibberd cites the letter by Owen on the day he called at his hotel:

> [He was] at his window in shirt sleeves, mooning. He received me like a lover. To use an expression of the Rev. H. Wigan's, he quite slobbered over me. I know not how many times he squeezed my hand, and, sitting me down on a sofa, pressed my head against my shoulder. [*two lines illegible*] It was not intellectual; but I felt the living verve of the poet ... who has fought *seventeen duels* (so it is said).   (Hibberd 168)

Owen may have succeeded in convincing his mother there was nothing erotic in Tailhade's behavior, and there was no sign that he responded positively. But to receive such a warm admiration from an eminent man of letters was, as Hibberd tells us, an experience for him to be treasured. Tailhade married twice; he lost his wife and baby a few years after his first marriage and got divorced from his second wife for his 'eccentricities' which resulted in the loss of his right eye at one time and the mutilation of his right hand at another. Many things concerning Tailhade should have stimulated young Owen greatly, but at the end of September he became calm again and returned to the natural compassion he had shown for the poor and suffering at Dunsden.

Along with the hint of Owen's homosexuality we know the importance of the literary influence of Tailhade upon Owen. He handed Owen two books: a copy of Flaubert's *La Tentation de Saint-Antoine* and a copy of Earnest Renan's *Souvenirs d'Enfance et de Jeunesse*. Tailhade thought them two of the greatest French classics of the nineteenth century. Owen read the two books with care, and found in them the spirit of that time and also the decadent, pre-modern literary inclination. Owen must have quickly strengthened the sense of the infinite and also the finite, which is his historical sense, at this time in the midst of the war. Germany had declared war against France on August 3.

> [Owen was] marking difficult words and interesting passages, including a remark by Renan that Celts can reach into a man's entrails and brings out secrets of the infinite. Like Wilfred and Tailhade, Renan had been of Celtic descent and brought up by a devout mother. (Hibbered 170)

While training for a priest Renan came to the conclusion that the Bible could not be literally true and this discovery became famous among French intellectuals. Renan's remark on the Celtic origin and the similar circumstance of his growing up surely made Owen feel safe and enlightened his career. The other book, Flaubert's *Tentation* was extraordinary mysterious and exquisitely composed. It was a great inspiration for Symbolist poets. The book was like a catalogue of the themes and imagery of French late-Romantic literature and art.

Owen's sonnets like *Storm* and *The End* are especially freshly influenced and vigorously challenging poems among his war poems.

第二章　ウィルフレッド・オウェン

Both poems begin with the images of great mythical worlds but the grand style soon reflects the stern reality of human death and the cruelty on the earth. The reader might expect a pastoral landscape but the poet laments in *Storm*,

>. . .
>
>I shall be bright with their [gods'] unearthly brightening.
>
>And happier were it if my sap consume;
>Glorious will shine the opening of my heart;
>The land shall freshen that was under gloom;
>What matter if all men cry aloud and start,
>And women hide bleak faces in their shawl,
>At those hilarious thunders of my fall?　　(8-14)

The poet presents a drama of his own death in the battlefield as another martyr, comparing himself to Jesus at his death. His lines are here emotionally decisive. The colloquialism of the last three lines makes the sorrowful heart of the poet get nearer to the readers', and the declarative addition to the preceding heroic statements increases his desperate sorrow. The line of women who 'hide bleak faces in their shawl' is a picture of despair. The skepticism of Christianity is frankly expressed in *The End*:

>After the blast of lightning from the east,
>The flourish of loud clouds, the Chariot-Throne;
>After the drums of time have rolled and ceased,
>And by the bronze west, long retreat is blown,

Wilfred Owen's War Poetry

> Shall Life renew these bodies? Of a truth,
> All death will be annul, all tears assuage?
> Fill the void veins of Life again with youth,
> And wash, with an immortal water, age? (1-8)

The scene of the Last Judgment is magnificently depicted but the glory of God would not be completed. Desperateness follows four questions one after another in front of "these bodies" and "the void veins" now with "all tears" of people. We find lamentation forced into the form of a classical sonnet, which is traditionally a form for love poems, and it was decorated with the sounds and words of half rhyme which is admitted as one characteristic of Owen's poetry. The repetitive use of the same vowels or consonants intensifies the poet's skepticism and agony.

Skepticism is one of the great elements of Owen's poetry, and it is to be developed into the famous expression of "the old lie". It is a critical phrase against the war. He is against the Latin propaganda: *Dulce et decorum est pro patria mori* (It is sweet and fitting to die for one's country). He fears moral infection but his duty as a poet is to express the extreme reality on the battlefield and to make the reader share his compassion. Siegfried Sassoon writes the memory of their days later and says that he only stimulated Owen toward writing with "compassionate and challenging realism." He confesses that the impulse within the younger poet had already been strong before their meeting. *Dulce et Decorum Est* is a 'gas-attack' poem and one of the four poems by Owen that readers are most likely to read.

> Gas! Gas! Quick, boys! – An ecstasy of fumbling,
> Fitting the clumsy helmets just in time;
> But someone still was yelling out and stumbling,

第二章　ウィルフレッド・オウェン

> And flound'ring like a man in fire or lime ...
> Dim, through the misty panes and thick green light,
> As under a green sea, I saw him drowning.　　(9-14)

He generates horror and accounts for this horror corrupting the flesh and the soul like this:

> If in some smothering dreams you too could pace
> Behind the wagon that we flung him in,
> And watch the white eyes writhing in his face,
> His hanging face, like a devil's sick of sin;
> If you could hear, at every jolt, the blood
> Come gargling from the froth-corrupted lungs,
> Bitter as the cud
> Of vile, incurable sores on innocent tongues, -　　(17-24)

He requires the reader to be a witness of the war through the mediation of the poem. The extreme expression of brutality on the battlefield needs no form as a vessel of fear but is just a sheer poem of true facts whose role is to cause compassion and pity. The images of suffering and agony are often depicted in detail. Owen's wide reading of English and European literature brings us to the comparison of his poetical images with those of Dante. Bergonzi cites from the recent book by Douglas Kerr and gives attention to his remark.

> Dante is the most bodily of poets and the fierce body language of the *Inferno* – there is not really anything like it in English – is also spoken in Owen's notations of intense staring, vivid and ghastly faces stretching out of arms, writhing rolling, flinching,

shrinking, clutching, wounding, and mutilation.

(Bergonzi, *War Poets* 21)

The Show has a similar setting to Dante and Virgil in *the Inferno*. It is an impressive poem of traveling by the poet [Owen] and Death.

> My soul looked down from a vague height, with Death,
> As unremembering how I rose or why,
> And saw a sad land, weak with sweats of dearth,
> Gray, cratered like the moon with hollow of woe,
> And pitted with great pocks and scabs of plagues.
>
> . . .
>
> I saw their bitten backs curve, loop, and straighten.
> I watched those agonies curl, lift, and flatten.
>
> Whereat, in terror what that sight might mean,
> I reeled and shivered earthward like a feather.
> And Death fell with me, like a deepening moan.
>
> And He, picking a manner of worm, which half hid
> Its bruises in the earth, but crawled no further,
> Showed me its feet, the feet of many men,
> And the fresh-severed head of it, my head.   (1-5, 21-29)

Kerr suggests that Owen learned from Dante that pain could be a subject for poetry, and the discovery would have given Owen a big step to start his career as a poet and some confidence to decide his theme, 'pity'.

The theme of pity and passive suffering in Owen's poetry seems to show the fact that it is a phenomenon of ultimate release of feeling and it belongs to the late Romanticism. It is opposed to T. S. Eliot's famous statement in 1919:

> Poetry is not a turning loose of emotion, but an escape from emotion; it is not the expression of personality, but an escape from personality. (Eliot 21)

Eliot's declaration is made at a time not so distant from Owen's struggle with his duty in the regiment and with his poems. Eliot lost his close friend in World War I, which made him write one of his famous early poems. But he had no experience on the battlefield himself.

Meeting Tailhade seems to have prompted Owen to explore his identity as a poet. He put off his return to England and enlistment in the regiment. Tailhade's lyrics tend to be derivative, but they were highly admired for his skill. Like other Decadents he was a fine craftsman and insisted on the need of music above everything. Avant-garde writers, including Ezra Pound and Richard Aldington in England, valued Tailhade as a satirist rather than as a lyricist. Though aggressively modern in some of his literary tastes, as Hibberd writes, he was also a devoted champion of the great writers of the past, and he was in some ways thoroughly traditional. Hibberd continues:

> He [Tailhade] believed poets should not try to create new kinds of feeling, as some of his contemporaries had wanted to do, but act as spokesmen for their age, working as hero-missionaries ― and if necessary martyrs ― in the undying cause of art and

> beauty. As for the war, he was as noisily patriotic, *cocoriquiste*, as anyone ... (Hibberd 173)

These lines are very interesting showing some important hints for understanding Owen's development in his art and life. While staying in France after meeting Tailhade, he tries to write an epic of Perseus, a Greek mythical hero, and imitates Verlaine, the Decadents, and others. Owen was obviously interested in 'hero' and 'heroism' like many other writers in wartime. His heroism is unlike the classical one, representing an anonymous soldier and his grief like in *Asleep*.

> Under his helmet, up against his pack,
> After the many days of work and waking,
> Sleep took him by the brow and laid him back.
> And in the happy no-time of his sleeping,
> Death took him by the heart.
>
> . . .
>
>
> Whether his deeper sleep lie shaded by the shaking
> Of great wings, and the thoughts that hung the stars,
> High pillowed on calm pillows of God's making
> Above these clouds, these rains, these sleets of lead,
> And these winds' scimitars;
> — Or whether yet his thin and sodden head
> Confuses more and more with the low mould,
> His hair being one with the grey grass
> And finished fields of autumns that are old ...
> Who knows? Who hopes? Who troubles? Let it pass!   (1-5, 10-19)

第二章　ウィルフレッド・オウェン

Owen's theme of pity and passive suffering is, desperately but persuasively, connected with this anti-heroism, and the compassion for other poor people had been nourished beforehand in the circumstance at his home and the vicarage. This change of theme from heroism to anti-heroism could be naturally brought from and intensified with his direct experience on the battlefield. Traditionally speaking in the field of literature, we can find the root of non-active capability in Keats' taste of poetry, 'negative capability'. Keats is a poet Owen admired from the beginning of his poetic career and Keats himself found the similar disposition in Shakespeare's works. The heroes at the front in the twentieth century are not like the classical heroes. They cannot see their enemies or their weapons with their eyes; they are not informed with the true cause or aim of the war. They don't know even the time of its ending. The modernization of weapons causing mass destruction and the rapid social change of nations toward the political, economical complexes deprived the ordinary people of their peaceful days and personal enjoyment in their individual lives. We can say that passiveness is forced on the citizens and it is the great theme to lament in the modern times. The war is fundamentally uncontrollable for the common people at least, and badly tragic in the modern highly civilized circumstances. Owen tries to write his poems with his particular theme of pity, and with anti-heroism which "was prefigured by Byron and Stendhal, and Sassoon and Barbusse" (Bergonzi, *Twilight* 120).

The other element besides sketicism in considering the attractiveness of Owen's poetry is the influence of the Decadents at the end of the 19th century. Tailhade was also a fervent admirer of Baudelaire and Gautier, and he had been a member of a group of young aesthetes himself in the 1880s. They had declared themselves 'Decadets' and claimed civilization had reached a cultural autumn. Morality and ideals were out of date, as Hibberd summarizes. It is interesting to point out that themes of passive suffering and smiling martyrdom constantly recur in the Decadent art, and pain and death were welcome as supreme sensations. Their aim included shocking the middle classes and they liked to associate themselves with anything that might cause outrage, notably homosexuality and sado-masochism. We can see a typical example of their assertion in the comment by Oscar Wilde: there is "no such things as a moral or immoral book. Books are well written or badly written." He is popular for his eccentric, controversial themes and expressions in his works. We are now drawn to "the wildest beauty in the world" that Owen continues to search for as a poet on the battlefield. He finds it in the extreme reality of human beings at the front. His images might have been hard, dry, concrete ones without the theme of pity. Beauty inseparable from extreme reality is described like this in *Greater Love*:

> Red lips are not so red
>   As the stained stones kissed by the English dead.
> Kindness of wooed and wooer
> Seems shame to their love pure.
> O Love, your eyes lose lure
>   When I behold eyes blinded in my stead!
>
> Your slender attitude
>   Trembles not exquisite like limbs knife-skewed,
> Rolling and rolling there
> Where God seems not to care;
> Till the fierce love they bear

第二章　ウィルフレッド・オウェン

　　Cramps them in death's extreme decrepitude.　　(1-12)

John Stallworthy shows in his book how Owen made use of *Before the Mirror* by Swinburne, one of the famous aesthetic poets at the end of the 19th century, and that Owen might have been aware of Salome's words to Jokannan in Wilde's *Salome*. "Red lips" could be read as a signification of sensual love, but it is reproved by the "greater love" of the soldiers and their sacrifice. "Greater love" originates from the sentence in John 15:13: "Greater love hath no man than this, that a man lay down his life for his friends." Owen represents the soldiers' great love in some horrible scenes. It leads to the terrible beauty of the soldiers' sacrifice. The didactic "greater love" is absorbed into the compassion of "the fierce love" at their death. The reality, schocking and sensual, as Jon Silkin says, might be Owen's intention in order to let the uninformed civilians know the condition of the doomed youth. On the other hand, *The Kind Ghosts* begins like this:

　　She sleeps on soft, last breaths; but no ghost looms
　　Out of stillness of her palace wall,
　　Her wall of boys on boys and dooms on dooms.

　　She dreams of golden gardens and sweet glooms,
　　Not marveling why her roses never fall
　　Nor what red mouths were torn to make their blooms.　　(1-6)

This poem dated July 30, 1918 shows the goddess of death, and the influence of the Decadents is recognized even in his great creative years: 1917-1918. Owen was brought to "a cruelly premature flowering in the hothouse of the Western front," and his work depicts something

131

of his fragility and brilliance. As Bergonzi admits of Yeats' criticism on Owen's diction that "his language was slower to develop than his sensibility, and wasn't always equal to his demands on it," we can find in this poem the familiar apparatus of the Tennyson/Swinburne images or some long languide syllables unsuitable for the dead soldiers' room. In *Anthem for Doomed Youth*, however, we realize some expressions of modernism that reveal his brilliant talent.

> What passing-bell for these who die as cattle?
>   – Only the monstrous anger of the guns.
>   Only the stuttering rifles' rapid rattle
> Can patter out their hasty orisons.
> No mockeries now for them; no prayers nor bells;
>   Nor any voice of mourning save the choirs, –
> The shrill, demented choirs of wailing shells;
>   And bugles calling for them from sad shires.
>
> What candles may be held to speed them all?
>   Not in the hands of boys, but in their eyes
> Shall shine the holy glimmers of goodbyes.
>   The pallor of girls' brows shall be their pall;
> Their flowers the tenderness of patient minds,
> And each slow dusk a drawing-down of blinds.　　(1-14)

Sassoon praises this poem in his *Siegfried's Journey* (1945) saying that this sonnet "confronted me with classic and imaginative serenity... and it was a revelation." He revised the Owen's original sonnet with no title more than five times, but it was a delightful collaboration for both of them while staying in the Craiglockhart War Hospital in Edinburgh in 1917.

This was one of "the two best war poems" Owen enclosed in the letter to his mother on September 25. It sprang from his experience reading an anonymous prefatory note in some anthology including a young poet who went to the front "singing to lay down his life for his country's cause." Stung by the sentiment and attacked by his remembrance at the Front just before, he wrote *Anthem,* but it might give the impression of retreat from his usual insistence on the soldiers' struggles and misery on the battlefield. Some critics note the contradiction between the protest of the first line and the rest of the thirteen lines, and Owen's purpose seems to be defeated. But, what is the greatest thing moving the reader through this poem? It should be sadness; sadness "with classic and imaginative serenity" as Sassoon describes and also a natural 'correlative' of sad feeling. Sadness loses its power with the word 'sadness' alone as Silkin says. We find the correlative of sad feeling loses a connecting word, copula, in the highest expression of his grief and anger. They are in the form of juxtaposition, which is the typical characteristic of the modernists' poetry. The first line reminds us of famous line by John Donne, one of the greatest metaphysical poets in the 17 th century, and some 'conceits' like in the last several lines are not connected with violence but with the representatives of compassion. Owen apparently comes nearer to the modernists' poetry in this poem. *Anthem* also shows a characteristic of Expressionism, emphasizing the eyes of the dead youth in the line: "in their eyes/Shall shine the holy glimmers of goodbyes." The irony disappears here, as if practicing what Eliot says "only those who have personality and emotions know what it means to want to escape from these things." Owen proceeds to the field of the modernists' poetry to show "the wildest beauty" in this world, mastering the world of aesthetic beauty at the end of the 19th century.

 Owen's sentiment might also be best understood through his

expression of nature. "Sad shires" in *Anthem* are the old homes in England which sent the young people off to the battlefields. They are no more the traditional pastoral world which means the place of the idealized life of countryside. *Spring Offensive* is the last poem written by Owen and it expresses nature as inseparable from human beings. The second and third stanzas generously use similes and metaphors and reflect the man's unity with nature.

> Marveling they stood, and watched the long grass swirled
> By the May breeze, murmurous with wasp and midge,
> For though the summer oozed into their veins
> Like an injected drug for their bodies' pains
> Sharp on their souls hung the imminent line of grass,
> Fearfully flashed the sky's mysterious glass.
>
> Hour after hour they ponder the warm field —
> And the far valley behind, where the buttercup
> Had blessed with gold their slow boots coming up,
> Where even the little brambles would not yield,
> But clutched and clung to them like sorrowing hands;
> They breathe like trees unstirred. (7-18)

The almost prosaic development of the poem, strewn with natural images, prepares a stage for the next battle. The little brambles which "clutched and clung to them like sorrowing hands" suggest the scene of the weeping people at the Crucifixion, and the soldiers who "breathe like trees unstirred" symbolize the desolate heroism with no alarms

> Of bugles, no high flags, no clamorous haste −
> Only a lift and flare of eyes that faced
> The sun, like a friend with whom their love is done.　　(22-24)

The objectivity of Owen's later poems could be said a measure to understand his maturity and the distance from his early romantic writings. The unity of human beings with nature claims the description of anger when nature faces the bloody destruction.

> ... And instantly the whole sky burned
> With fury against them; earth set sudden cups
> In thousands for their blood; and the green slope
> Chasmed and steepened sheer to infinite space.　　(29-32)

The religious metaphor gives readers the dark anticipation with the deepest sorrow, and the panorama of the merciless battlefield is brought before our very eyes. These lines are quite the opposite of those in the first stanza where the soldiers

> ... fed, and lying easy, were at ease
> And finding comfortable chests and knees,
> Carelessly slept　　(2-4)

surrounded by the great nature. *Spring Offensive* was sent to Sassoon unfinished and the last stanza is added later in a pencil, but the last two stanzas depict and clearly show the sacrificial nature of the soldiers' suffering as in the line: "some say God caught them even before they fell." And the last stanza emphasizes the few survivors who are deadly mute and filled with paradox of their existence.

> The few who rushed in the body to enter hell,
> And there out-fiending all its fiends and flames
> With superhuman inhumanities,
> Long-famous glories, immemorial shames –
> And crawling slowly back, have by degrees
> Regained cool peaceful air in wonder –
> Why speak not they of comrades that went under? (40-46)

Only a few survivors who come back from the hell know and can tell the truth, but they keep a secret about the paradox of their courage with "superhuman inhumanities" and their glories with 'immemorial shames.' The last line is a question, but the essential movement of the last two stanzas is toward 'warning' as in Owen's preface. Nature is used here as the means to criticize human beings' behavior and the poem is coming near to a traditional category of allegory.

In concluding Wilfred Owen's War Poetry, the problem of celebrity and universality of Owen's war poetry reminds us of the saying by C.M. Bowla about the experiments of modern poetry: poetry moves between allegory and mystery, and his words suggest that poetry includes, more or less, both of them. Pity is the core theme and sentiment of Owen's poems, and his poetry is in the category of allegory in a sense that it evokes a specific feeling and conveys a special meaning. It signifies and represents allegory of war. Owen must have realized his poetical challenge through his reading the works by Dante. Dantean description full of wonder and reality in *the Inferno* could lead him to and make him write his preface. Through many poetical experiments Owen reaches the highest level and expresses "the wildest beauty in the world." He represents the suffering and agony of many anonymous soldiers on the battlefields and reveals the deception in his contemporary world. The extremity of his poems, also, seems to succeed in creating a vision like in *Strange Meeting*.

> Foreheads of men have bled where no wounds were.
> I am the enemy you killed, my friend.
> I knew you in this dark: for so you frowned
> Yesterday through me as you jabbed and killed.
> I parried, but my hands were loath and cold.
> Let us sleep now...'   (39-44)

The emotion of pity in his war poems has not only 'objective correlative' to escape from emotion, but a vision leading to a poetical truth of his own making. The richness of his poetry, allegorical and also mysterious, is intensified with his core factor: pity. His elegiac and monodramatic poetical style was encouraged by Sassoon, and the appreciation by some contemporary writers only a few months before his death could set Owen in the position of a martyr to beauty. In London in July 1918, Owen heard Sassoon was in hospital after being shot in the head, which "changed everything" (Hibberd 411). Owen decided that if Sassoon was no longer able to speak for the troops, another poet would have to stand in for him. Owen wrote to his mother that "now I must throw my little candle on his torch, and go out again," enclosing Sassoon's letter and referring to him as 'the greatest friend' he had. Owen died just one week before the end of World War I. It would not be too much to say that his destiny recalls the Oscar Wilde's death in 1900 in France as a martyr to beauty after two years of penal servitude for homosexuality without any legal protest. Owen's short life often stimulates people to write his biography, and many letters to his family, especially to his mother, are good materials to investigate his days still further. Owen's poetry shows that he is a traditional and transitional poet at the beginning of the twentieth century when there existed various artistic experiments as well as the last light of Romanticism. His pity, beauty and horror still excite us when we read his poems, and the thrill of excitement is the beginning of understanding poetry. "No commentary will reveal to us its secret" as Eliot says in the note of introduction for *In Parenthesis* by David Jones, another contemporary war poet.

Reference Books
Bergonzi, Bernard. *Heroes' Twilight*. (Carcanet Press Ltd., 1965 third ed. 1996).
──. *War Poets and Other Subjects*. (Ashgate, 1999).
Bloom, Harold. Ed. *Poets of World War I*. (Chelsea House, 2002).
Eliot, T.S. *Selected Essays*. (Faber & Faber, 1972).
Hibberd, Dominic. *Wilfred Owen*. (London: PHOENIX, 2002).
Jones, David. *In Parenthesis*. (Faber & Faber, 1975; Eliot's introduction, 1961).
Kendall, Tim. *Modern English War Poetry*. (Oxford, 2006).
Motion, Andrew. *Keats*. (Faber & Faber, 1997).
Silkin, Jon. *Out Of Battle*. (Macmillan, 1998).
──. *Wilfred Owen: THE WAR POEMS* (London: Chatto & Windus, 1996).
　　(All citations of Owen's poems are to this edition.)
大平真理子　『英国の戦争詩人たち』　荒竹出版　2001.
草光俊雄　『明け方のホルン』　みすず書房　2006.
清水一嘉編　『一次大戦とイギリス文学』　世界思想社　2006.
C.M. バウラ　『現代詩の実験』　大熊栄訳　みすず書房　1981.
──. 『象徴主義の遺産』　小林忠夫訳　篠崎書林 1975.

Wilfred Owenの戦争詩と
"the Instant Maturity Legend"

　Wilfred Owenが戦死するまでの最後の二年間に集中して優れた詩を残していることはよく知られているが，Andrew Motionは彼のエッセイ集，*Ways of Life*（2008年）の中の一篇，*The Last Two Years*の中でそれを"the instant maturity legend"とよび，その不思議について解明を試みている。

　MotionはまずOwenの伝記作者でもあるJon Stallworthyの*Life*（1979）に言及しながら，Owenの詩人としての成熟の旅を'a smooth and harmonious development'であるとしたStallworthyの解釈に疑問を呈した数少ない人の一人にPhilip Larkinを挙げている。MotionはすでにLarkinについての詳細な伝記，*Philip Larkin, A Writer's Life*（1993）を書いているが，その中でLarkinがOwenについての伝記的事実を付け加えていることに注目している。LarkinはStallworthyによるOwenの伝記の書評の中でRobert GravesとRobert Rossに関する事実を付け加え，書評が公開された後，Stallwortby自身に宛てて手紙を書いている。Robert GravesはOwenとの関係が深いSiegfried Sassoonと交流があり，Robert RossはOscar Wildeとの関係と裁判で当時有名だった。その手紙の中で，彼は「Owenには同性愛の直接の証拠はないが，当時それは犯罪であり，また同時にあまり知られていなかった，という二つの点を忘れてはいけない。」（Motion, *Larkin* 65）と述べ，Owenの同性愛と戦争詩との関係はE. M. ForsterやChristopher Isherwoodの場合にもみられると言っている。またLarkinは，「これはその結果生じた芸術作品が低く評価されるということではない」（66）と断っている。

　次にMotionはDominic Hibberdの大著であるOwenの伝記，*Wilfred*

Wilfred Owenの戦争詩と "the Instant Maturity Legend"

 Owen（2002）の詳細で慎重な書き方に触れ、HibberdはOwenが'homosexual'であると一度も言及できず、そしてその明確な証拠がないことに身動きできないでいると述べ、Hibberdは大げさと思われるほど、それについての正確な証拠と言明を避け、詳細な伝記を書き続けていると指摘する（Motion, *Ways* 215-6）。彼はまた、Stallworthyもすでに注目していたことだが、Owenが1913年にフランスに渡ったとき知った詩人であり作家であるフランス人のLaurent Tailhadeとの出会いと彼の文学その他についての影響力の強さについて述べ、のちに、Owenの弟であるHarold Owenによって否定され続けることになるWilfredとの性的な特別な関係の始まりも示唆している。1917年のCraiglockhart戦争病院でのSiegfried Sassoonとの出会い以前に、Owenには同性愛に関連した環境が準備されていたということができる。

 MotionはOwenが戦争病院を後にした1917年末から彼の詩に革命が起きたと述べ、主題である兵士は戦場の死傷者という存在ではなく崇めるべき肉体を待った男であり、どの詩をとっても詩人が伝えるのは存亡の危機にある 'male companions' についての喜びの感覚であると言っている。それはHibberdが伝記の中で明らかにしているように、Craiglockhart戦争病院にOwenが到着する直前の戦場での彼の惨状からは全く想像のつかない世界だが、Motionは次のように書いている。

> Owen having fought in France for the first four months of 1917, is about to go to Craiglockhart. A brave warrior-poet, reprieved from slaughter? Hardly. Owen has recently been accused of cowardice by his commanding officer, and is now jittery, plagued by nightmares, angry with his existing circle... and at the same time unable to discover either people to replace it or an adequate language in which to speak his mind. (Motion, *Ways* 217)

第二章　ウィルフレッド・オウェン

戦場での英雄とは程遠く，shell-shockの患者としてエジンバラの戦争病院に入ったOwenは，治療の過程で自然観察や雑誌の編集に関わりながら戦争の悪夢から遠ざかることになる。そして，フランス人Laurent Tailhadeとの出会いが同性愛の入り口としての出来事であるとすれば，1917年の８月からのSiegfried Sassoonとの交流は，Tailhadeの場合に勝る影響力を持った，彼の戦争詩人としての地位を確立する大事件だった。*The Dead-Beat*はOwenがSassoonのもとを離れて間もなく，一人でSassoonのスタイルで書き，何度も書き直した一篇であるが，そこには先輩詩人の反戦の訴えや教訓主義とは違った独自のリアリズムが存在する。

  A low voice said,
'It's Blighty, p'raps, he sees; his pluck's all gone,
Dreaming of all the valiant, that *aren't* dead:
Bold uncles, smiling ministerially;
Maybe his brave young wife, getting her fun
In some new home, improved materially.
It's not these stiffs have crazed him; nor the Hun.' (ll. 9-15)
    ［詩の引用はすべてStallworthy版（1994）による］

  低い声がした，
「内地送還だ，たぶん，彼もわかっている。戦意を失くしている，
英雄たちのことを夢見ているんだ，死んでいない奴らさ，
大臣のように笑っている不敵なオジキたちのことさ。
素晴らしい彼の奥さんかもしれない，
手を加えてよくなった新しい家なんかで楽しくやっているんだ。
彼を狂わせたのはこういった死体じゃないさ，ドイツ野郎でもない」と。

この詩は，当時Sassoonの詩に頻繁に用いられていた口語体を採用し，戦場での一場面を一幕の劇にすることで，本国には届かない戦地での真実

Wilfred Owenの戦争詩と"the Instant Maturity Legend"

をうたっている。Jon Silkinはこの詩は「共感の詩人Owenが辛辣な、皮肉な、また風刺の詩も書けることを思わせる」(*Owen* 11-12) と述べ、また、Owenの最後の詩とされる *Smile, Smile, Smile* では、前半で、当時の労働党党首やフランスの首相、クレマンソーの言葉が詩の素材として用いられ、後半ではそれに対する傷痍軍人の沈黙を通して戦争への欺瞞が提示されていることから、彼が「政治的な話も消化して詩にする能力を持っていることを示している」(12) と詩集の注釈で述べている。

このように、詩人としてのOwenは様々な詩を書くことのできる才能に恵まれていたと考えられるが、MotionはOwenの有名ないくつかの詩は、特にその苦痛が同情だけでなく官能的に描かれているからますます激しい感情を呈しているのだ、と言って、'*I saw his round mouth's crimson*' の断片を引用している。Owenの詩人としてのあまりにも早い成熟のカギを握るものとして、Motionは伝記によって明らかにされる事実とOwenの文体の変化の時期の一致を示唆しながら、二人の詩人、TailhadeとSassoonに共通する資質、そしてLarkinも指摘した同性愛を挙げて、次のようにこの評論を終えている。

> When Owen identified his true, strong homosexual self, he discovered his genius. When he lost contact with the earth, he was vulnerable. (221)

MotionはOwenの戦争詩は彼が自らのアイデンティティーを探し当て、解放と自信に裏打ちされて生み出されたものであると結論付ける。また、Hibberdの伝記が明らかにしているひとつの事実に触れ、ボートで運河をわたる途上で撃たれて亡くなる直前のOwenは、ヘラクレスによって大地から持ち上げられ倒される前の不死身のアンタイオスのように、部下を鼓舞する士気衰えぬ兵士であったと語っている。

Owenの戦争詩につきまとう"the instant maturity legend"の不思議については、特に母親宛てに多く書かれ、しかも弟のHaroldによって部分

第二章　ウィルフレッド・オウェン

的に処分されたとされる書簡集への関心を中心に，さらに興味深い研究がなされている。重要なことは，Larkinが断っているように，伝記で解明される事実によって芸術作品が低く評価されるということではなく，その事実を統合してもなお，その普遍性が維持され，鑑賞が深まるかどうかということであろう。

　Owenは出版予定だった詩集の序文に有名な「詩は憐憫の中にある」という一文を書いているが，「私は詩を重視していない，主題は戦争であり，戦争の哀れである」と断言することを可能にした環境や心情は作品の中にまず求めることができると思われる。

　Hibberdの伝記によれば，Craiglockhart戦争病院で書かれたもっとも興味深い二つの作品である*Dulce et Decorum Est*と*Disabled*はOwenがSassoonを知る前に書いた作品を書き改めたものであり，ロマン派詩人やデカダンの詩の愛好者であったOwenの過去は決して無駄にされてはいない。概して，Owenは詩作に慎重で，入念に何度も書き直している場合が多い。では，憐憫を主題とし，すでに認められつつあった自分の詩について，「私は詩を重視していない」と断言した意味は，そして"the instant maturity legend"との関係はどこに隠されているのだろう。Motionの結論を踏まえながら考えてみたい。

　Owenの戦争詩を肉付けする重要な構成要素の主なものを挙げるとすれば，それらは，ロマン派や世紀末芸術の美意識であり，ダンテを始めとする古典文学の叙事詩の構造であり，キリスト教に対する懐疑と反戦の考え方であると言えるだろう。実に多彩である。憐憫を核としてこれらの要素を自由に取り込みながら，Owen独自の世界が展開されている。ここでは，古典文字に言及，またはそれを下敷きにした詩について考えてみたい。

　Stallworthyによって1994年に編集され，出版されたOwenの56篇の詩の中に*Schoolmisteress*という詩がある。

　　Having, with bold Horatius, stamped her feet
　　And waved a final swashing arabesque

143

Wilfred Owenの戦争詩と "the Instant Maturity Legend"

> O'er the brave days of old, she ceased to bleat,
> Slapped her Macaulay back upon the desk,
> Resumed her calm gaze and her lofty seat.
>
> There, while she heard the classic lines repeat,
> Once more the teacher's face clenched stern;
> For through the window, looking on the street,
> Three soldiers hailed her. She made no return.
> One was called 'Orace' whom she would not greet. (ll. 1-10)

大胆不敵なホラチウスに合わせて足を踏み鳴らし,
古代の勇敢な日々に向けて最後のポーズをピシャリときめると,
彼女は哀れっぽい口調をやめて,
マコーレーの本をパシッと机の上に戻し,
静かな視線に戻り,自分の高い席に着いた。

そこで,古典の数行が繰り返されるのを聞いている間にもう一度,
彼女の顔が険しく引き締まった。
通りに面した教室の窓越しに,
三人の兵士が彼女に呼びかけたからだ。彼女は何も返さなかった。
一人はホラチウスと呼ばれたが,彼女は挨拶しようとしなかった。

Owenが戦争病院に入院中の1917年の秋に,治療の一環として体験した小学校での授業の経験をもとにその冬に作られたものと推測される作品である。マコーレー作の『ホラチウス』を教える女教師の,出兵する教え子に対する心の矛盾を描き出しているが,その皮肉な設定は戦時下では珍しくなかった光景に違いない。ホラチウスについてはもちろんOwenの有名な詩である*Dulce et Decorum Est*の題名にも採用されている。Sarah Coleはその著書, *Modernism, Male Friendship, and the First World War*の中で,

第二章　ウィルフレッド・オウェン

19世紀のパブリック・スクールや大学の数の驚くべき増加や質の変化に触れ，19世紀半ばから第一次世界大戦までの長期にわたる年月の間の古典教育や，教育機関における男性コミュニティや絆の構築，さらにホーマーからホプキンズに至るまでの同性愛の歴史について概観しているが，この詩では戦時下のヒロイズムの風潮を背景にした一人の女性の心の動揺が映し出されている。引き裂かれた心を静かに描き切ることによって生まれるこの詩の哀しみとアイロニーは，同じホラチウスの詩句から取った*Dulce et Decorum Est*では，Owenが同じ序文の中で「一詩人が今日できることは警告することぐらいだ」と述べている「警告」に変わっている。

> If in some smothering dreams you too could pace
> Behind the wagon that we flung him in,
> And watch the white eyes writhing in his face,
> His hanging face, like a devil's sick of sin;
> If you could hear, at every jolt, the blood
> Come gargling from the froth-corrupted lungs,
> Obscene as cancer, Bitter as the cud
> Of vile, incurable sores on innocent tongues, –
> My friend, you would not tell with such high zest
> To children ardent for some desperate glory,
> The old Lie: Dulce et decorum est
> Pro patria mori.
> (ll. 17-28; Silkin 版は7行目の"Obscene as cancer,"を略している)

もしこの世とは思えぬ息もつけぬ夢の中で
我々が彼を投げ入れた荷馬車の後ろについて君も歩くことができるなら，
顔面で見もだえする彼の白い目を，
罪に嫌気のさした悪魔のような，彼の垂れ下がった顔を見ることができるなら，
もし君が振動のたびに，気泡が壊れた肺から血が

145

Wilfred Owenの戦争詩と"the Instant Maturity Legend"

  ゲボゲボと音をたてて出てくるのを聞くことができるなら，
  腫瘍のように見苦しい，反芻された食物のように苦い，
  けがれない舌に不快な癒しがたい苦痛を残す血だ―
  友よ，よもや君は意気高揚して言いはしまい
  瀕死の栄光とやらがほしくてたまらない子供たちに
  あの古い大嘘を，甘美でうるわしい
  祖国のために身を捧げるは，と。

この毒ガスの詩はSilkinによると，Owenの詩の中で最も読まれている四つの詩のうちのひとつであり，戦争の大義名分を真正面から糾弾した反戦詩である。道徳的，倫理的汚染の怖さが肉体の破壊の描写を通して読者に突きつけられている。abab cdcd efefと押韻され，もともと恋愛をうたった定型詩であるシェイクスピア形式のソネットで書かれているが，最後の二行連句は書かれず，それを待たずして，この詩の意図する警告の目的はすでに達成されている。戦場での肉体の破壊の現実と恐怖を創造し，Owenの戦争詩を代表するものの一つになったこの詩は，Owenの詩に共通する顕著なひとつの特徴を持っている。Santanu Dasは彼の著書，*Touch and Intimacy in First World War Literature* (2005) の中で「Owenにとっては読むことも書くこともきわめて肉体的なことだった。」(138) と述べ，Owenの成熟した詩の特徴は苦痛と演劇性であると分析している。

> Pain and theatricality characterize the body in Owen's mature poetry. If, in Sassoon's *The Redeemer* or Blunden's *Undertones of War,* soldiers are realized as tiny dots against the landscape, with Owen, it is this contorted body that defines space. (152)

Santanu Das は，StallworthyやHibberdも触れてはいるが，Owenの書簡集に多く見られる病気や肉体の痛みの表現について興味深い考察をしている。Dasによると，Owenは従軍前にも次々に手紙の中で苦痛の表現を交

えて最新の不快感を母親に報告しており，それはHypochondria（心気症）であり，それについての「際限のない共感や感情移入は母と子の間の秘密の絆」であった。さらに，「幼少期と思春期の度重なる病院通いによってOwenは驚くべき肉体の知識と親密性を得た」のだ，と述べている。それは弟のHaroldも回顧する「兄の健康への病的な没頭ぶり」からも推測でき，「気泡の壊れた肺からゲボゲボと音を立てて出てくる血」という描写の生々しさや特異性との観点からも十分に理解できることである。Dasはまた，Owenの心気症をFreudの理論を応用して説明している。心気症は自己陶酔症と強い結びつきがあり，病気のように苦痛や痛みとなって発症し，無意識の罪悪感から生じる病気や心気症をFreudは'moral masochism'と結びつける。DasはこれまでOwenの研究で見過ごされてきたのは肉体的苦痛と詩を書くことの親密な結びつきであり，詩の中で苦痛と喜びが身体のどこか一部に特に集中して書かれていることを指摘する。さらに官能的な表現を増した代表的な作品として*Greater Love*が挙げられる。

> Red lips are not so red
>   As the stained stones kissed by the English dead.
> Kindness of wooed and wooer
> Seems shame to their love pure.
> O Love, your eyes lose lure
>   When I behold eyes blinded in my stead!
>
> Your slender attitude
>   Trembles not exquisite like limbs knife-skewed,
> Rolling and rolling there
> Where God seems not to care;
> Till the fierce love they bear
>   Cramps them in death's extreme decrepitude. (1-12)

Wilfred Owenの戦争詩と "the Instant Maturity Legend"

  赤い唇もこれほど赤くはない
    死んだイギリス兵士にキスされ汚れた石ほど。
  求愛され,求愛するもののやさしさも
  彼らの純粋な愛に比べれば面目もない。
  恋人よ,君の目も魅力を失う
    私の代わりに見えなくなった両目を私が見るとき。

  君がそのほっそりしたポーズで震えても
    あそこでのたうちまわっている
  ナイフのように曲がった身体のようにうまくはいくまい,
  そこは神も知らん顔だ。
  ついには彼らが背負う熾烈な愛が彼らを痙攣させるのだ
    死の究極の衰弱の中で。

Sassoonが嫌った'ecstasy'という言葉を使うことなく,Owenはそれを兵士の死の瞬間として具体化し,戦場での究極の愛の存在を描くことで独自の憐憫の世界を創り上げる。肉体的苦痛と詩を書くことの親密な結びつきはさらに叙事詩の構想の中で,より俯瞰的な視点から書かれた詩にもみられる。

  My soul looked down from a vague height, with Death,
  As unremembering how I rose, or why,
  And saw a sad land, weak with sweats of dearth,
  Grey, cratered like the moon with hollow woe,
  And pitted with great pocks and scabs of plagues.

  Across its beard, that horror of harsh wire,
  There moved thin caterpillars, slowly uncoiled.
  It seemed they pushed themselves to be as plugs

Of ditches, where they writhed and shriveled, killed. (*The Show* ll.1- 9)

私の魂はかすむ高台から,「死」とともに見下ろした,
どのようにして,なぜ上ってきたかのは思い出せないのだ,
そして悲しい土地を見た,飢饉で流した汗で弱り果て,
灰色で,虚ろな嘆きで月のようにくぼみができ,
そして伝染病の大きなあばたやかさぶたができていた。

そのあごひげのような　残酷な恐怖の鉄条網を横切って,
痩せた毛虫が数匹動き,ゆっくりとまるめた全身を伸ばした。
身体を投げ出し,溝の栓になるのかと思われたが,
そこで彼らは身をくねらせ,身を縮め,死んだ。

Bernard Bergonziが指摘しているように,苦痛が詩の主題になりうるということをOwenはダンテから学んだ。そして,Dasが書簡集の中で見出したようにOwenはKeatsに心酔することによって,Keatsの燃える心に触ることで詩を書くことを始めた。それらを統合したこの詩では,ウェルギリウスやダンテが体験した地獄めぐり,そして死に教えられるという一種の古典叙事詩の手法を取り入れて,Owenは戦場の恐怖を小さな生物を通して描いている。そして,この戦場のパノラマと殺戮の恐怖を客観的で詳細な観察力と特異な比喩によって描くことで,この詩はOwen独自の叙事詩となっている。

　官能的な詩から叙事詩まで幅広い詩を書いていたOwenは興味深いことに,戦争に生き残ることができた場合を想定した計画を書き残している。James Fentonは*The Strengh of Poetry*（2001）の中で,その計画の中にウェールズをテーマにした自由詩劇や,すでに書き始めていたペルセウスの愛の詩の再開も含まれていることを指摘し,詩人としてのOwenが年代的に順当に調和した段階を進んでいたのではなく,彼の優れた作品が書かれた２年足らずの期間に,多くのことが彼の心のうちに秘められていたと

Wilfred Owenの戦争詩と "the Instant Maturity Legend"

述べている。Owenは終戦の一週間前に戦死している。彼の戦争詩は従軍する彼にとって，それらが第一義的に戦争や戦争の哀れを主題としているから大事であり，当時，詩そのものは問題ではなくなっていた，いや，少なくとも，そう断言できるほど彼には自信があったと推測できる。彼には詩を書く目的があり，彼はその意義を信じていた。伝記の事実からも裏付けされるように，彼にはすでに当時の文学仲間との交流や詩の出版の道が開かれていた。それまで彼を悩ませていた性の問題や，詩人としての野望や宗教の悩みが詩の中に感じられることはあるが，戦場での真実と兵士の哀れを書くことで，自分が背負ってきた過去とある意味で決別し，自由で自信に満ちた彼独自の世界を築くことができたと言える。彼にとって愛や，死，神，恐怖，歓喜といった詩の主題は戦争によって命を吹き込まれ，その輝きを増すことを彼は知った。今，ここに戦争があることが彼にとって何よりも優先された。しかし，英雄の話でもなく，名誉や権力の話でもない，平凡な一市民が参加した近代の世界戦争の真実と哀れをうたうこと，それがOwen独自の戦争詩の魅力であり，ヒューマニズムを訴える強さの源泉となったのだ。戦争がOwenに詩を放棄させ，戦争がOwenを詩人にしたのだと言えるのではないだろうか。"the instant maturity legend" は戦争を契機にロマン主義の残像や世紀末の文学の潮流を一気に駆け抜けたOwenが残した短くも太い生の軌跡が生み出したものと言える。

参考文献

Bergonzi, Bernard. *War Poets and Other Subjects* (Ashgate, England, 1999).

———. *Heroes' Twilight* (Carcanet, Manchester, 1996; first published 1965).

Cole, Sarah. *Modernism, Male Friendship, and the First World War* (Cambridge, 2003).

Das, Santanu, *Touch and Intimacy in First World War Literature* (Cambridge, 2005).

Fenton, James. *The Strength of Poetry* (Oxford, 2001).

Hibberd, Dominic. *Wilfred Owen, A new Biography* (Phoenix, London, 2003).

Hipp, Daniel. *The Poetry of Shell Shock* (McFarland, North Carolina, 2005).

Kendal, Tim. *Modern English War Poetry* (Oxford, 2006).

Motion, Andrew. *Ways of life, On Places, Painters and Poets* (Faber, 2008).
——. *PHILIP LARKIN, A Writer's Life* (Faber, 1993).
Silkin, Jon. *Wilfred Owen, The War Poems* (Chatto & Windus, 1994).
——. *Out of Battle, The Poetry of the Great War* (Macmilan, 1998). (first Oxford edition 1972).
Stallworthy, Jon. *Wilfred Owen* (Oxford, 1974).
——. *Wilfred Owen, The War Poems* (Chatto & Windus, 1994).
荒木映子.『第一次世界大戦とモダニズム』世界思想社　2008.
清水一嘉.『第一次世界大戦とイギリス文学，ヒロイズムの喪失』世界思想社 2006.

第三章

フィリップ・ラーキン

ANOTHER MASK

—— In the Case of Philip Larkin ——

1. Toward the real world

The Movement was first given a popular definition at the almost same time as Larkin finished *The Less Deceived*. Andrew Motion says that it seems to have accelerated his development toward an unmistakebly English ideal[1]. He points out that the most important and character-forming tensions in Larkin's poetry are between an undeceived pessimism and a wishful-thinking optimism, though Larkin has often been regarded as a hopeless and inflexible pessimist by many critics and poets. Motion also finds symbolists effects and devices indispensable in the poet's literary development.

Philip Larkin, the representative of the Movement Poets in 1950's, gives us many aspects of living after the World War, depicting apparently domestic, solitary, sometimes patriotic, everyday life. It might be clear that one of his great characteristics in poetry, which shows a certain direction in the world of English poetry after the war, is the style of writing about empirical existence of man. It is contrasted with the psychological insight or mythological heroism as the characteristics of the modernism. It may appear to be non-dramatic, much static and skeptical:

How overwhelmingly persuades

ANOTHER MASK

> That this is a real girl in a real place,
> In every sense empirically true!
> Or is it just *the past?*[2)]   (24-27)
>
> *(Italics* are Larkin's)
> from *Lines on a Young Lady's Photograph Album*

These lines are far from the anti-heroic mentality of Prufrock, whose overwhelming question disturbing the universe leads to the hesitation and undecision. Larkin admits the girl's photo as a real world in a real past, as she lies there 'unvariably lovely there.' She and that moment are true and real, and also eternal. *Lines* appears at the beginning of his second anthology, *The Less Deceived.* It is significant not only because it shows his own poetical style, but because it suggests his place as a poet after the war and the modernism. He knows himself separated from the past, being 'at exclusion.'

> We know *what was*
> Won't call on us to justify
> Our grief, however hard we yowl across
>
> The gap from eye to page.[3)]   (33-36)
>
> *(Italics* are Larkin's)

We can find Larkin's writing style of empirical existence of man already in his first volume, *The North Ship.*

> XXVI
> This is the first thing
> I have understood:

> Time is the echo of an axe
> Within a wood.[4]

Here we know the poet released from the ordinary world and time-bound everyday life in the modern sorroundings. This is a moment of his discovering of the real time in the real world: a true moment beyond time. Thise lines are very simple and easy to understand. It might not be called inspiration, but he is sure at the door of the *real* world.

2. Imagination *into* the real world

It is generally admitted that the two big effects on Larkin's poetic career are through W.B. Yeats and Thomas Hardy. We can see something called the Yeatsian transcendentalism or Hardy's resignation in many poems in *The North Ship*; and many critics admit Larkin's pessimism under the Hardy's view of life and fate still after the first anthology. But that is all that Larkin communicates? Andrew Motion steps further into the style and the making of Larkin's poems. He says:

> His response is certainly not Yeats's heroic struggle to rise
> above time, but neigher is it Hardy's shoulder-shrugging
> acceptance of fate.[5]

In the autobiographical talking, Larkin admits the three years writing like Yeats "out of infatuation with his music," and says it is "not because I liked his personality or understood his ideas."[6] Motion tells us his start as a poet with their shadows which remain in his poetry in other poetical form.

Motion's second mark is that Larkin often takes a form of question or debate. He sees the skepticism at the bottom of his thoughts, as well as the straightforwardness of the real world he depicts. To make it more precise, it is possible to say that he has had a kind of anger or indignation to the life ever since the beginning of his poetic career. *The Dancer* in the first anthology, for example, has the destructive picture under the predominance of Yeats' lines.

> And if she were to admit
> The world weaved by her feet
> Is leafless, is incomplete?
> . . .
> Then would the moon go raving,
> The moon, the anchorless
> Moon go swerving
> Down at the earth for a catastrophic kiss. (1-3, 7-10)

The order of the universe depends on her (dancer's) ability of recognition of or judge on what is *real*. Some assumptions and doubts in *The North Ship* proceed to the anger in the second volume. He is struggling for an empirical solution which follows the insight into life. *Toads* is one of the most popular poems of Larkin's, because the symbolic use of toads as workers (labourers) is shocking to show the enslaveness to the work in the modern world. But he is moderate and hesitates to choose the way of escape or transcendence. He knows now he must stay here in this world and we should accept both of the two contradictory answers in order to resolve the conflict of life.

> Why should I let the toad work
>   Squat on my life?

> Can't I use my wit as a pitchfork
> 　And drive the brute off?
> ...
> I don't say, one bodies the other
> 　One's spiritual truth;
> But I do say it's hard to lose either,
> 　When you have both.[7]
> 　　　*Toads*　　(1-4, 33-36)

This conclusion sounds to be one after the long consideration of human conditions in this world and this bitter answer shows one of the great characteristics of Larkin's poetry. It reveals a kind of compromise in the midst of struggle for self-justification. And his resentment and self-contempt we can find again in the third volume, *The Whitsun Weddings*. His understanding of the meaning of life is that it is 'first boredom, then fear.' His view of life, of course, is not the religious one like T.S. Eliot's.

> Why did he think adding meant increase?
> To me it was dilution. Where do these
> Innate assumptions come from? Not from what
> We think truest, or most want to do:
> Those warp tight-shut, like doors.[8]
> 　　　*Dockery and Son*　　(34-38)

Facing the death of his old friend, Larkin retrospects their lives. Their choices are different, leaving his friend with a son and nothing to himself. What he concerns with is why people would have a family, which, he says, could be a forced habit and a suddenly hardened life-style. His struggle has a long way to the reconciliation with life and strikes a note of unsettlement in this world. Larkin's imagination, however, catches 'something hidden from us' and he discloses our ignorance.

> Strange to know nothing, never to be sure
> Of what is true or right or real,
> But forced to qualify *or so I feel*,
> Or *Well, it does seem so:*
> *Someone must know.* [9]
>   *Ignorance*   (1-5)
>
>   (*italics* are Larkin's)

The poet is honest to declare it is 'strange' to feel nothing certain, nothing real and all our life spent on imprecision. His understanding of human conditions is that 'our flesh/Surrounds us with its own decisions' and he comes to define that love is our almost-instinct, almost true, and love is 'what will survive of us.' Here is no ancient myth, no mythical heroism in the literary tradition. Larkin's imagination *into* the real world makes us know about the world made up of many assumptions and hypotheses. We feel something as something because we feel like that, and because 'it does seem so.' We don't know what is real and 'someone transcendent must know' it. His answer for the best way of reconciliation with the world, he holds back till the last, fourth anthology, *High Windows*. His resentment and skepticism are searching for the "not seeming" world. The empirical self itself denies self-deception, only left with the imaginative jump to the transcendence. We know at this point Larkin has the same surroundings as the French symbolists had over a half-century ago.

3. "Catching happiness"

Motion's criticism focuses on the symbolist devices in Larkin's poetry and some other critics also find the effect of Mallarmé on the title poem of the Larkin's last mature anthology.

> Rather than words comes the thought of high windows:
> The sun-comprehending glass,
> And beyond it, the deep blue air, that shows
> Nothing, and is nowhere, and is endless.[10]   (17-20)

The lines like 'The sun-comprehending glass,/ And beyond it, the deep blue air' still anticipate his commitment to the world, but two negative words, 'nothing' and 'nowhere' or a sense of freedom of 'endless' suggest the shift of nature of his poetry 'from grumbling, ironical, colloquial speech to symbolist intensity.'[11]   Motion stresses on the significance of Larkin's symbolist devices throughout his career, which may suggest the remains of Yeats' effects. Many critics including Motion let us notice the traditional inheritance in Larkin's works. The poet, however, was reluctant to admit it and did not always agree to this point except owing to Hardy. He has his own pursuit of empirical self in his works, too. It is one of the characteristics of the poets living in the post-war England. We realize now it is what Motion calls 'an unmistakably English ideal'.

> 'Without the aid of fertility rituals or the collective unconscious, he (Hardy) has shown how the provincial can become the universal.' This more directly human approach to literature is presented as characteristically English, and a possible source of

161

vitality for the future.[12]

Motion's greater pointing out about Larkin's poery is, however, that the poet is never separated from the literary movement and effects of the modernism. (It might remind us of Eliot's famous sentences in *The Tradition and the Individual Talent*.) In spite of Larkin's reluctance to admit the experience reading symbolist works, his style sometimes shows jump from the argument or discarding of the syntax of discourse. It helps the pursuit of empirical self gain an indispensable quality of poetry: an imaginative power of transcending.

The nature of his earlier works is an ironical grumbling about unsatisfaction and uneasiness of his everyday life. His moon, for example, is 'so definite and bright,' but 'hurts the eyes.' 'The moon is full tonight' but it appears for him to have 'drawn up/ All quietness and certitude of worth,' 'For they are gone from the earth.'[13] The moon is a common and familiar subject to sing with. Its brightness and clearness, however, make him reflect his inner self. Using the traditional romantic image, it intensifies his complaint. The prosaic speech expressing his repressed agony is looking and yarning for the appearance of his own Muse.

> If I can keep against all argument
> Such image of a snow-white unicorn,
> Then as I pray it may for sanctuary
> Descend at last to me,
> And put into my hand its golden horn.[14]
> *The North Ship* (xx, 52-56)

But 'tender visiting,/ Fallow as a deer or an unforced field'[15] remains uncertain as before and the poet makes deeper his insight into life through the empirical consideration of self in the next volume. He outgrows the monotonous pessimism in the first anthology to hold a new intensity and a new field of transcendence. He catches a symbolic taste and a metaphysical sensitivity in a poem like *Absences*. The following three stanzas show a gradual transformation from natural description of the sea to the stability of some building, and from the 'pinned' vastness of the sea to the joyous surprise of discovering the absence of grumbling himself.

>Rain patters on a sea that tilts and sighs.
>Fast-running floors, collapsing into hollows,
>Tower suddenly, spray-haired. Contrariwise,
>A wave drops like a wall: another follows,
>Wilting and scrambling, tirelessly at play
>Where there are no ships and no shallows.

>Above the sea, the yet more shoreless day,
>Riddled by wind, trails lit-up galleries:
>They shift to giant ribbing, sift away.

>Such attics cleared of me! Such absences![16]   (1-10)

It is himself that 'tilts and sighs' and he is a vast spreading sea. The movements of ever-changing sea and the tireless waves are painted like a piece of picture. They are suddenly hardened into solid images of walls and ribbing of a giant building. And without knowing it the complaining, half-personified sea is away and transformed into 'attics' which has entirely cleared of him. He has no normal relationship between concepts and things in his mind and such symbolist devices make it possible for him to have a transformtion of his conflicts. By means of his poetic imagination he could transform the bleakness of his mind. This is his way of assertion of freedom from the pursuit of the empirical self and it is a rare experience for him;

> by liberating him from the familiar, circumscribed world, they (the symbolist devices) allow him to experience and convey a sense of transcendence.[17]

Abscences is a poem catching the moment of happiness when he could experience a sense of transcendence. The poem is celebrated with the end rhymes like sighs, Contrariwise, or hollows, follows, shallows, or play, day, away, or shift, sift, and with the echoes of alliteration like wave, wall, or ships, shallows, shift. The light-hearted devices convey and intensify the liberation of his mind. The moment of happiness could be said the moment when the bleakness of his mind has turned into an 'objective correlative,' through which he could communicate his world in an artistic form.

Reviewing his earlier works, Larkin ironically says that 'the real world was all right providing you made it pretty clear that it was a symbol.'[18] But the imaginative excitement after the symbolist strategies, or imaginative jump to the another world beyond the empirical surroundings like in *Absences*, does not gurantee a positive or enduring release of his mind. He is careful and guards himself against the usage and definition of imagination, especially related to the field of poetry he is interested in.

Very little that catches the imagination can get clearance

from either the intelligence or the moral sense. And equally, properly truthful or dispassionate themes enlist only the wannest support from the imagination. The poet is perpetually in that common human condition…[19]

Considering the process of making the poem we could find the subtlety or ambiguity in the last line in *Absences*. It communicates not only the surprise of disappearance of grumbling himself, but reveals his unexpected joy of trascendence beyond the world. The last line is unnecessary if he is satisfied with himself absolutely free from the world after the artistic completion of the solid image of his inner desolation. It has extra exclamatory sentences. We can remember now the skillfullness and strategies of E. Pound, such as bold cuttings or reconstructions he has done to the original drafts of Eliot's works. Whether a work is artistically superior or not depends, for Pound at that time, "on no leaks of emotion as it is." But pure objectivity and symbolist transformation are not the last aims for Larkin, as well as for Eliot. Larkin's unique poetical style lies in the expression of *transient* release of mind from the bleakness of his mind living in this world. The setting forth both art and emotion reflects the style after the symbolist movement and in the post-modernism. The entire reliance on the particular romantic imagination, which is based on refinement of ideas or abstract concepts into the utmost intensity of expression, is solely the symbolists inclination. And the difficult games of recherché themes are the modernists' products as they exclude emotions.

Absences is thus a very interesting poem from the artistic point of view and also from the historical development of poetry in England after the world war. Larkin, the representative of the Movement poets, put the Movement's democratic manner into practice. In his poems, the poet is removed from a garret or ivory tower and put firmly on the street; it was, in Alvarez's words, 'an attempt to show that the poet is not a strange creature inspired; on the contrary, he is just like the man next door – in fact, he probably *is* the man next door.'[20]

(*italics* is Alvarez's)

Larkin was, however, to depart from the Movement's orthodoxy in many poems. It is a paradox that his greatness was recognized after the publication of his second volume, *The Less Deceived*, in which he shows his characteristics of the pursuit of the empirical self and also the temporary transcendence after the symbolists. The symbolist soaring helps his lines about this world have another intensity and depth. When he began to present his own style, he was recognized as the first of the Movement (orthodox) poets. An ironic, self-critical *persona* created in the poems like *Toads* or *Lines on a Young Lady's Photograph Album* in the anthology of *The Less Deceived* appeals to the people who experienced the war and expected the freedom from the struggle of life. His poetry is a mask in the street, not in a high-brow, intellectual group. It was not necessary for him to make 'a continual extinction of personality' and his mask was welcomed with the poems including the lines of passing intensity of transcendence after the symbolist devices.

4. Mask in the post-modernism

According to the C.G. Jung's definition in his psycho-analysis, *persona* is the outer personality opposed to *anima:* the inner personality. We cannot find the apparent division of Larkin's personality in his poems, because he seems to know well about the entire-skepticism in which the symbolist writers were involved. For them *reality* is absolutely not in this world. Larkin's experience reading Yeats' works makes him familiar with the literary situation after the war;

> Something of that Romantic-Symbolist distrust of the 'real' and 'objective' world was carried over into Yeats' maturity, into the long quarrel between his empirical self and his 'anti-self,' between the circumstantial and the archetypal. Out of that quarrel he did indeed make magnificient poetry...[21]

Larkin has to take a way different from Yeats' in order to grasp and present truth in this life as a new poet. He has no heroes, myths, nor Byzantium. His poems are the very mask of himself who has nothing but empirical self and half symbolist strategies. Larkin's pursuit of the empirical self, which includes rare experience of transcendence, could be said to have made up a complete mask of himself. His mask is a mask in the street, but very delicate. It is impossible for him to jump and soar eternally like a romantic poet, because

> Time has transfigured them (the earl and countess) into
> Untruth. The stone fidelity
> They hardly meant has come to be
> Their final blazon, and to prove
> Our almost-instinct almost true:
> What will survive of us is love.[22]

It is not time that makes human beings possible to transcend the world. The stone has fidelity revealing what is almost-instinct is almost true.

Love may be only one which survives beyond time, but Larkin does not quite agree to his own conclusion. The stone fidelity has fixed the image of love between them by making a shape of holding one hand with the other's. What is 'a sharp tender shock' for the poet is that love is also unbeliebable without some kind of experience with one's own eyes. Time shows only those which are empirically true through the stone's fidelity. The last two lines suggest the transient glow of love in this world against the darkness of skepticism. Larkin suspects the reality in this world has to include love, because without love he has nothing but 'the deep blue air, that shows/ Nothing.' Larkin's poetry is his mask to show and not to show his reality deprived of love through his pursuit of the empirical self. It is a *real,* fleshy, mask in the period of post-1945. This exquisite quality is one of the so-called ideal Englishness. Larkin is a Movement poet.

NOTES
1) Motion, Andrew. *Philip Larkin* (London: Methuen, 1982), 77.
2) Larkin, Philip. *The less Deceived* (London: The Marvell Press, 1977), 13.
3) Larkin, *Deceived* 14.
4) Larkin, Philip. *The North Ship* (London: Faber & Faber, 1979), 39.
5) Motion, 70.
6) Motion, 33.
7) Larkin, *Deceived* 33-34.
8) Larkin, Philip. *The Whitsun Weddings* (London: Faber & Faber, 1971), 38.
9) Larkin, *Whitsun* 39.
10) Larkin, Philip. *High Windows* (London: Faber & Faber, 1981), 17.
11) Motion, 81.
12) Faulkner, Peter. *Modernism* (London: Methuen, 1985), 71.
13) Larkin, *North* 14.
14) Larkin, *North* 33.
15) Larkin, *North* 48.
16) Larkin, *Deceived* 40.

17) Motion, 75.
18) Motion, 73.
19) Motion, 72.
20) Motion, 31.
21) Michael Hamburger, *The Truth of Poetry* (London: Methuen, 1982), 72.
22) Larkin *Whitsun* 46.

REFERENCES

Baudelaire, C. *BAUDELAIRE Selected Writings on Art & Artists* translated by P.E. Charvet (Cambridge University Press, 1981).

Davie, Donald. *Purity of Diction in English Verse and Articulate Energy* (London: Penguin, 1992).

Booth, James. *Philip Larkin Writer* (Harvester Wheatsheaf, 1992).

King, P.R. *Nine Contemporary Poets* (London: Methuen, 1979).

Eliot, T.S. *Collected Poems* (London: Faber & Faber, 1970).

Eliot, T.S. *Selected Essays* (London: Faber & Faber, 1972).

Eliot, T.S. *The Waste Land A Facsimilie & Transcript of the Original Drafts* (London: Faber & Faber, 1971).

後書き

　本書の題名を考えるにあたって，「現代英詩を訪ねて」や「現代英詩の旅」がうかんだ。これまで，つれづれに書き溜めてきたものを振り返ってみると，詩を読むことは私にとって，新しい世界の発見であり，未経験の感動であって，どちらかといえば研究より旅に近いと感じたからである。モダニズムの名前も知らず，無謀にもT.S.エリオットの詩をはじめとする現代詩の旅に出たのが遠い昔のことになってしまった。考えてみると来年は第一次世界大戦が勃発してから百年になる。現代詩の中核となったモダニズムの実験的作品が多く生まれた時代には，文学にとどまらず，絵画や音楽の世界でも多くのエポックメイキングな作品が創られたが，そこには戦争を背景にした時代の大きなうねりがあった。その時代の文化を掘り下げながら，それぞれの作品を解明していく作業はまだまだ'overwhelming question'と言えるのかもしれない。

　20世紀の英詩壇の巨人であるT.S.エリオットが危機の時代の詩人・文化人として，自身のエグザイルの旅を記録したといえるならば，英国を一度も出ることなく，かつ桂冠詩人の席を辞退したフィリップ・ラーキンの人生は，市井の一人間がひとり生という虚実を突き抜ける旅であり，生への郷愁ではなかったか。また，20世紀という世界戦争の時代を象徴するかのような戦争詩人ウイルフレッド・オウエンは，憐憫を核として極限状態の兵士の姿を詠い続け，その短い旅は私たちを文明の原点に連れもどした。

　これらの詩人の作品をどれだけ多く，どれだけ深く読みこなせたかをお話できる自信など全くないが，私の詩の旅は私の中にある種の安堵と手応えを残してくれたことは確かである。拙著には思いがけない誤解や曲解が含まれているかもしれない。ご叱責を賜れば幸いである。

　エリオットの詩の演習をきっかけに私を詩の旅に導いてくださった学部時代の中村幸士郎先生，大学院で古今の英詩を国際的な視点からご教示く

ださった湯浅信之先生，シェイクスピアを現代から読み解いてくださった故松元寛先生他，たくさんの先生や友人にお世話になった。心から感謝申し上げたい。また，本書の出版に際し，本務校である名古屋経済大学から研究費の一部を使用させていただいたことを記しておく。最後になったが，例年にない酷暑の中，不揃いな論文のために大変お手数をおかけした木村斉子さんをはじめ溪水社の皆様に厚く御礼申し上げる。

　付記　　私事ながら，出版を後押ししてくれた夫にこのささやかな書をささげたい。

　2013年　盛夏

中元　初美

人名索引

A
アンドルーズ　Andrewes, Lancelot (1555-1626)　83-85, 88, 92, 93
オールデイントン　Aldington, Richard (1892-1962)　127
アリストテレス　Aristotle (384-322 B.C.)　97

B
バルビュス　Barbusse, Henri (1873-1935)　129
ボードレール　Baudelaire, Charles Pierre (1821-67)　7, 27, 33, 46, 47, 60, 71-74, 89, 129
バーゴンジー　Bergonzi, Bernard　117, 119, 125, 129, 132, 149
ブランデン　Blunden, Edmund (1896-1974)　146
バウラ　Bowra, C.M　43, 136
ブラドレー　Bradley, F.H.　101
ブルトン　Breton, Andre (1896-1966)　66
ブッシュ　Bush, Ronald　38, 39, 54, 82, 83, 88, 89, 91, 109, 110

C
クレマンソー　Clemenceau, Georges (1841-1929)　142
コーガン　Coggan, Donald　106
コール　Cole, Sarah　144
コルビエール　Corbiere, Tristan (1845-1875)　40, 43, 46-48, 61, 62, 64, 65, 69, 89

D
ダス　Das, Santanu　146, 147, 149
デイビー　Davie, Donald　38, 39, 62, 63
ダン　Donne, John (1572-1631)　31, 42, 84, 88, 89, 133
ダンテ　Dante, Alighieri (1265-1321)　42, 108, 126, 136, 137, 143, 149
ドストエフスキー　Dostoyevsky, Fyodor Mikhaylovich (1821-81)　7
ドルー　Drew, Elizabeth　99, 108

E
エリオット　Eliot,Thomas Sterns (1888-1965)　5-8, 14, 16, 20, 26, 27, 127
エンプソン　Empson, William (1906-84)　119

F
フェルチ　Felch, Susan M.　86
フェントン　Fenton, James　149
フロベール　Flaubert, Gustave (1821-1880)　122
フロイド　Freud, Sigmund (1895-1982)　9, 147
フォースター　Forster, E.M. (1879-1970)　139

G
ガードナー　Gardener, Helen　40, 42
ゴーチエ　Gautier, Theophile (1811-1872)　74, 130

173

ゴードン　Gordon, Lyndall　98
グレイブス　Graves, Robert (1895-1985)　139

H
ハーデイ　Hardy, Thomas (1840-1928)　7, 157, 161
ハリス　Harris, Daniel　91
ヒバード　Hibberd, Dominic　121, 127, 128, 130, 137, 139, 140, 143, 146
ホーマー　Homer　145
ホプキンズ　Hopkins, G.M. (1844-89)　145
ヒューム　Hulme, Thomas Earnest (1883-1917)　78

I
イシャウッド　Isherwood,Christopher (1904-86)　139

J
ジョイス　Joyce, James (1882-1941)　48, 49, 84
ジョンストン　Johnston, John H.　117
ジョーンズ　Jones, David (1895-1974)　138
ジョーンズ　Jones, Genesias　46

K
キーツ　Keats, John (1795-1821)　6, 129, 149
カーモード　Kermode, Frank　97
カー　Kerr, Douglas　125, 127
ナイト　Wilson Knight　97, 99

L
ラフォルグ　Laforgue, Jules (1860-87)　7-10, 14, 15, 20, 26, 33, 36, 38, 39, 44, 46-48, 50, 65, 66, 89
ラーキン　Larkin, Philip (1922-85)　139, 142, 143, 155-168
リーヴィス　Leavis, F.R.　14
レーマン　Lehman, David　34, 35

M
マコーレー　Macaulay, T.M. (1800-1859)　144
マラルメ　Mallarme, Stephane (1842-98)　6, 36, 38, 41-43, 46, 47, 52, 55, 57, 79, 89
マックナイト　McKnight　110
メドカーフ　Medcalf, Stephen　82, 83
ミルトン　Milton, John (1608-74)　42
モンロー　Monroe, Harriet (1860-1936)　121
ムーデイ　Moody, A.D.　111
モーション　Motion, Andrew　139, 142, 143, 155, 157, 161, 162,

N
ニューボルト　Newbolt, Sir Henry　117-119
ニーチェ　Nietzsche, Friedrich (1844-1900)　103

O
オウエン　Owen, Wilfred (1893-1918)　117-138, 139-150
オウエン　Owen, Harold　142

P
パターソン　Patterson, Gertrude　84

パース　Perse, St. John　85
ペルセウス　Perseus　128, 149
ピカソ　Picasso, Pablo Ruiz (1881-1973)　5
ポー　Poe, Edgar Allan (1809-49)　7, 50, 65
パウンド　Pound, Ezra (1885-1972)　8, 9, 27, 41, 61, 78, 127, 165

R

ルナン　Renan, Earnest (1823-92)　122
ランボー　Rimbaud, Jean Arthur (1854-91)　9, 27, 46
ランセ　Rince, Dominique　61, 62
ロス　Ross, Robert　139
ラッセル　Russell, Bertrand (1872-1970)　30

S

サスーン　Siegfried, Sassoon (1886-1967)　119, 121, 124, 129, 132, 133, 135, 137, 139-143, 146, 148
スカーフ　Scarfe, Francis　33-34
セネカ　Seneca (4?B.C.-A.D.65)　99, 101-104
シェイクスピア　Shakespeare, William (1564-1616)　111
シェレー　Shelley, Percy Bysshe (1792-1822)　6
シルキン　Silkin, John (1930-97)　117, 120, 131, 142, 146,
スミス　Smith, Grover　31, 69
ストルワジー　Stallworthy, John　131, 139
スタンダール　Stendhal, Henri (1783-1842)　129
スウインバーン　Swinburne, A.C. (1837-1909)　131, 132
シモンズ　Symons, Arthur (1865-1945)　6, 61

T

テラード　Tailhade, Laurent　120, 121, 127-129, 140-142
テインマーマン　Timmerman, John H.　82, 87, 90-93, 96, 99, 106

U

上田保　(1894-1980)　5
ジョイス　Joyce, James (1882-1941)　48, 49, 84

V

ヴァレリー　Valery, Paul (1871-1945)　7
ベルレーヌ　Verlaine, Paul (1844-96)　128
ウエルギリウス　Virgil (70-19B.C.)　126, 149

W

ウオレン　Warren, Charles　97
ウイガン　Wigan, the Reverend Herbert　120, 121
ワイルド　Wilde, Oscar (1854-1900)　5-6, 130, 137, 139
ウルフ　Woolf, Virginia (1882-1941)　88

Y

安田章一郎　(1914-)　8
イエーツ　Yeats, William Butler (1870-1957)　7, 119, 132, 157, 158, 161, 167

〈事項・作品　その他〉

A
アレキサンドラン　alexandrine（弱強六歩格）69-71, 74
allegory　寓意　136
アニマ　anima　166
アバンギャルド　avant-garde　127

B
バウラ　C.M.Bowra著　『象徴主義の遺産』43, 136
biblical symbolism　91
ブランデン　Edmund Blunden（1896-1974）作品：*Undertones of War*　146
ベアトリーチェ　Beatrice　108
ベルリッツ語学学校　the Berlitz School of Languages　120
'boredom, terror and glory'　43
ボードレール　Charles Pierre Baudelaire（1821-67）の作品：「万物照応」*Correspondences*　72-73
ボルドー　Bordeaux　120

C
「クラーク・レクチャーズ」*Clark Lectures*　38
the Craiglockhart War Hospital　133, 140, 143
繋辞　copula　38, 39, 63, 133
ケルト　Celts, Celtic descent　122
コルビエール　Tristan Corbiére（1845-1875）の作品：
「黄色い恋」62, 65
「コルビエールの墓碑銘」67, 80
コーガン　Donald Coggan著：*The Heart of the Christian Faith*　106
コンシート　conceit　133
コール　Sarah Cole　著：*Modernism, Male Friendship, and the First World War*　144
colloquialism　123
内包　connotation　46

D
ダイアナ　Diana　97
Dantean colour symbology　87
ダンテの「煉獄編」*Purgatory*　95, 104, 105
ダンテの「地獄編」*Inferno*　125, 136
ダス　Santanu Das　著　*Touch and Intimacy in First World War Literature*　146
デカダン　Decadents　127-131, 143
discursive　34, 39
Desdemona　103
ドッペルゲンゲル　9
dramatic monologue　50
明示　denotation　46

E
エリオット　Thomas Sterns Eliot（1888-1965）の作品：
The Tradition and the Individual Talent　8-9, 162

The Love Song of J.Alfred Prufrock
  8-9, 13, 61, 62, 78
Conversation Galante 10-11, 14,
  44
Autre Compainte de Lord Pierrot
  11-12
Humouresque 16-18
Nocturne 18-19
Rhapsody on a Windy Night 20-29
The Waste Land 27, 28, 31, 41,
  42, 48-51, 54, 56, 63, 66-68, 77-
  79, 82, 84, 101, 105
The Waste Land Facsimilie 41, 63
The Fire Sermon 48, 49
Mr.Apollinax 29-32
Burnt Norton 38, 55-56, 99, 107
Dry Salvages 38
Four Quartets 38, 41, 43, 51-54,
  62, 93
East Coker 54
Little Gidding 50, 53, 74
Baudelaire 41, 61, 71
Ash-Wednesday 43, 53, 79, 96,
  98
Morning at the Window 44-45
Cooking Egg 62
Hamlet 63
Le Directeur 64-65
Complainte-Épitaphe 66
Mélange Adultére de Tout 67
  Lune de Miel 68-69, 74
  Dans le Restaurant 69, 75-78
  Reflection on Vers Libre 70-71
  The Hollow Men 79, 84, 96, 98
  Ariel Poems 83, 98
  A Song for Simeon 96, 110
  Animula 96, 110

Journey of the Magi 83, 85, 88,
  91, 96, 98, 110
Marina 95, 96, 98, 99-101,
  104, 106, 110-112
Coliolan 96
Unfinished Poems 96
*Shakespeare and the Stoicism of
  Seneca* 103
empirical self 160, 161, 164, 166-
  168
epiphanic experience 95, 112, 166
enjambment 句またぎ 70
English ideal 155
Expréssionism 表現主義 133

F

フォーム form 41, 42, 49, 50, 53,
  65, 72, 79
フロベール Gustave Flaubert (1821-
  80) の作品：
  La *Tentation de Saint-Antoine* 122
フェントン James Fenton 著 The
  Strength of Poetry 149
French Symbolists 160

G

Gower 110

H

Hercules 102-104
Humility 103
hero, heroism, 英雄 128, 150
Hypochóndria 心気症 147

I

ideal Englishness 168
イマジズム imagism 27, 78

イマジスト　imagist　8
インカネーション　incarnation　50,
　86, 89, 90, 93
呪文　incantation　39, 43, 53, 55,
　56, 111
incantatory power　85
invocation　喚起　39, 46, 52, 56

J
juxtaposition　並列　133
ジョーンズ　David Jones（1895-1974）
　の作品：
　In Parenthesis　138
ジョイス　James Joyce（1882-1941）
　の作品：
　Ulysses　48, 49, 84
ヨハネ　Saint John of the Cross　90
ヨハネの福音書15章13節：　John 15:13
　131

K
King's Chapel　98
古典主義者　60
Wilson Knight著　*The Wheel of Fire;
　Myth and Miracle*　97, 99

L
ラーキン　Philip arkin（1922-85）の作品：
　*Lines on a Young Lady's Photograph
　　Album*　155, 156, 166,
　The Less Deceived　155, 156, 166
　The North Ship　156-158, 162
　The Dancer　158
　Toads　158, 166,
　The Whitsun Weddings　159
　High Windows　160
　Absences　163-165

ラフォルグ　JulesLaforgue（1860-87）
　の作品：
　「月の出の前の会話」　7
　「ピエロたち」　20
レーマン　David Lehmanの作品：
　Perpetual Motion　「不断の運行」
　34, 35

M
mad poetics　36, 44
マラルメ　Stéphane Mallarmé（1842-
　98）の作品：
　「詩の危機」　52
　「音楽と詩」　54
the Movement　155
the Movement Poets　165
メイカー　maker　5, 8, 28, 32, 42
モダニスト　modernist　79, 45, 133
モダニズム　modernism　34, 39, 53,
　155
モーション　Andrew Motion著
　Ways of Life　139
　The Last Two Years　139
　Philip Larkin, A Writer's Life　139
moral masochism　147

N
negative visionary　54

O
オウエン　Wilfred Owen（1893-1918）
　の作品：
　*The Parable of the Old Man and the
　　Young*　118
　Storm　123
　The End　123
　Dulce et Decorum Est　124, 143-145

Asleep 128
Greater Love 130-131, 147-148
The Kind Ghosts 131
Anthem for Doomed Youth 132-134
Spring Offensive 134-135
Strange Meeting 137
The Dead-Beat 141
Smile, Smile, Smile 142
I saw his round mouth's crimson 142
Disabled 143
Schoolmistress 143-144
the Oxford Book of Modern Verse (1936) 119
Othello 103
撞着語法 oxymoron 107

P

パース St. John Perseの作品：
　Anabase 85
paradox 136
煉獄 *Purgatory* 111
Peripeteia 98
pity 憐憫 127, 136, 137, 143, 150
ペリクレス Pericles 97, 98, 100, 102, 104-106, 109-111
persona 仮面 9, 16, 48, 166
ポエトリー誌 8
ポスト・モダニズム post-modernism 33, 53, 56, 165

R

バラ園 rose garden 54, 99, 107
ルナン Earnest Renan (1823-92) の作品：
　Souvenirs d'Enfance et de Jeunesse 122

リアリズム realism 5, 48
recognition scene 96, 97, 99, 100
Roman stoicism 103
Romantic-Symbolist 167
ロマン主義 60

S

懐疑主義 skepticism 123, 124, 143, 160, 168
サウザム B.C.Southam 107
サスーン Siegfried Sassoon (1886-1967) の作品：
　Siegfried Journey 132
　The *Redeemer* 146
サンボリスト 60-65, 70
象徴主義 サンボリスム symbolism 5, 6, 8, 9, 27, 28, 38, 56, 61, 63-65, 78, 79, 88, 89
『象徴主義の文学運動』 6, 61
シェイクスピア William Shakespear (1564-1616) の作品：
　Pericles 96, 97, 100
　Othello 103
　Macbeth 107
'Shakespearean Rag' 51
Shakespear's parable 95
象徴 symbol(s) 46, 72, 86, 91, 99
スウインバーン A.C.Swinburne (1837-1909) の作品：
　Before the Mirror 131, 132
水死 45, 78
ストルワジー John Stallworthy著：
　Life 139
セジューラ（行中の休止） 70
セネカ Seneca (4?B.C.-A.D.65) の作品：
　Hercules Furrens 99, 101-104

ソネット　sonnet　48, 71, 74, 145

T

「ターンブル・レクチャーズ」
　　Turnbull Lectures　54
テインマーマン　John H. Timmerman
　　著
　　*T.S.Eliot's Aeriel Poems: The
　　Poetics of Recovery*　96
テラード　Laurent Tailhade著：
　　Lettre aux Conscrits;　121
　　Pour la Paix　127

V

ビジョン　vision　40-43, 46, 48, 50,
　　53, 54, 56, 99, 106, 137

W

第一次世界大戦　World War I　117,
　　120, 127, 138
第二次世界大戦　World War II　155
ワイルド　Oscar Wilde（1854-1900）
　　の作品:
　　Salome　131, 138, 139

【著者】

中元　初美（なかもと　はつみ）

略歴　広島大学大学院文学研究科英語学英文学専攻
　　　博士課程後期単位取得満期退学
　　　現在　名古屋経済大学教授
著書　『ウイルフレッド・オウエン戦争詩集』
　　　英宝社2009　（翻訳）
論文　「イースト・コーカーにみる幻視の人」他
翻訳　フィリップ・ラーキン著「北を往く船」,
　　　エドワード・トマス著「詩集」,
　　　アンジェラ・カーター著「紫の上の恋」,
　　　「死刑執行人の美しい娘」,「日本のお土産」他

現代英詩を読む
──エリオット，オウエン，ラーキンの作品を中心に──

平成25年9月20日　発行

著　者　中元　初美
発行所　株式会社　溪水社
　　　　広島市中区小町1－4　（〒730-0041）
　　　　電話082-246-7909／FAX082-246-7876
　　　　e-mail: info@keisui.co.jp
　　　　URL: www.keisui.co.jp

ISBN978-4-86327-231-6　C3098
©2013 Printed in Japan